THE KING AND THE TUTOR
FABLES FOR OUR TIME

MICHAEL ROSEN
ILLUSTRATED BY TIM SANDERS

www.michaelrosen.co.uk/books

CONTENTS

Their Fault	5	Very Mysterious	28
Stop	6	Rebels	29
Sanctity	7	Mistakes	30
Demands	8	Liars and Hypocrites	31
A Map	9	A Special Day	32
In the Way	10	Swordsmanship	33
Critics	11	Science	34
Horrible Things	12	Principle	35
Looking into it	13	No Longer Our Friends	36
Killing all the Mice	14	Love	37
Good Wars	15	Do as You Would . . .	38
Waging War	16	History	39
In Charge	17	Unworthy	40
Tit for Tat	18	Badness	41
Dealing with it	19	Borders	42
The Enemy	20	Hope	43
Bad Stuff	21	A Pet	44
The Palace	22	An Experiment	45
Fiercely Independent	23	False Friends	46
Title Deeds	24	Suffering	47
Since	25	The Problem	48
Drastic Measures	26	What Next?	49
Homework	27	Are Our Enemies Human?	50

Friends	51
Normal People	52
Rich	53
What's Necessary	54
We've Finished	55
To Protect People	56
Children	57
Scribes	58
Chess	59
A Restraining Influence	61
The Right People	62
Tournaments	63
The Emperor	64
A Safe Place	65
It's Going Well	66
Letters	67
Ironic	68
The Council	69
Judges	70
Outrage Wars	71
Glee	72
Boasting	73
Controlling the Situation	74
Consequences	75
Situations	76
Bad People	77
Traitors	78
Damage	79
The Future	80

Crimes	81
Most People Don't Understand	82
How Will it End?	83
The Solution	84
Punishing People	85
Modern Times	86
Pain	88
Negotiations	90
Truth	92
Divided	93
Atrocities	94
We Don't Know . . .	96
Successful	97
Agenda	98
Have I Got This Right?	99
Grave Concern	100
Deeply Concerned	101
Ancestral Lands	102
When Does History Begin?	103
How to Look Away	104
The King Over-There	106
Something Monstrous	107
Nothing	108
Flat	109
Objectives	110
Crocodiles	111
Hardly Anyone Will Notice	112
The Thing About War	113
Nutrition	114

Being Bad	115	Pictures	146
Day One	116	Concern	147
People	117	The News	148
Escalation	119	Saving Lives	150
Some People Are Hurting	121	A Greater Power	151
Condemnation	122	Position	153
A Truce	123	Excellent Weapons	154
Looking Good	124	A Secret Weapon	155
The Only Way	125	Attack is Defence	156
Bing-Bangs	126	On the Brink	157
What it Looks Like	127	Names	158
Actions	128	Reports	160
Prying People	129	Good People	162
Kind People	130	Values	163
Starving People	131	A Proclamation	164
Numbers	132	Civilisation	165
Are We Bad?	133	A Mess	166
An Announcement	134	The Correct Answer	168
The Right Thing	135	Other Motives	169
Framing	136	Supreme Power	170
Words and Deeds	137	The Moon	171
Missing the Point	138	Talking to the Enemy	172
A Very Humane War	139	The Emperor's Job	174
Power	140	People in the Way	176
Busybodies	141	Bad Scribes	178
Peace	142	Peace Treaty	179
Vagueness	143	Long-term Objectives	181
That Corner	144	Highly Moral People	182
Last Chance Saloon	145		

INTRODUCTION

This book was inspired by another book: *The Prince* by Niccolò Machiavelli which first appeared in 1532. It's a book that has had a huge influence ever since and one example of this is of course that we have the word 'machiavellian', meaning someone who is scheming and plotting, for their own selfish ends, often in order to get or keep power over someone else or others.

In fact, that's not quite what *The Prince* is about. It's a book that seems on a first reading to be advice from Machiavelli to a prince on how to rule. It's possible to read it as if it's a straightforward, realistic – probably cynical – set of guidelines: a kind of self-help guide for ruthless rulers.

Others have read it as being subversive: that these aren't real guidelines but an exposé of how the modern ruler of that time was ruling, and that Machiavelli was revealing to those being ruled just what was going on. After all, the 16th century was a time of huge change in how rulers were ruling. The old ties of feudalism with its complex arrangements about obligations between the rulers and ruled were breaking apart. Shakespeare represents this in the clash between the Earl of Gloucester and his son Edmund in the play *King Lear*. Gloucester represents the old 'natural' world and Edmund is the scheming 'machiavel' upsetting what the old world regarded as 'legitimate'. Edmund is Gloucester's son but he is a bastard in both senses of the word. Here's Gloucester talking to Edmund, wondering what's going on, what's going on with the 'natural' order:

> 'These late eclipses in the sun and moon portend no good to us. Though the wisdom of nature can reason it thus and thus, yet nature finds itself scourg'd by the sequent effects. Love cools, friendship falls off, brothers divide. In cities, mutinies; in countries, discord; in palaces, treason; and the bond crack'd 'twixt son and father. This villain of mine comes under the prediction; there's son against father: the King falls from bias of nature; there's father against child. We have

seen the best of our time. Machinations, hollowness, treachery, and all ruinous disorders follow us disquietly to our graves. Find out this villain, Edmund; it shall lose thee nothing; do it carefully. And the noble and true-hearted Kent banish'd! his offence, honesty! 'Tis strange.'

Edmund mocks all this from the point of view of being a bastard.

Now, I put these thoughts and 'sources' together and wondered, what if there was some kind of dialogue I could invent that had one foot in the 16th century and the other foot in the 21st, inspired by Machiavelli's *The Prince* and Shakespeare's *King Lear* but applied to the cynical and ruthless ways of thinking and talking going on right now?

So I came up with *The King and the Tutor*, with the King inspired in part by Gloucester, and the tutor by Machiavelli and Edmund.

I've published most of these dialogues on Facebook and some people have wondered whether they are about one political situation or several. I'm agnostic about that. They were written in 2023 and 2024. A lot's been going on. If you want to apply these dialogues to specific goings-on in the world, then I am more than happy you do so. If you think that they are about non-specifics, more general about how rulers rule, then again, I'm happy about that too.

One suggestion about reading them: you might find that the best way to do this is to read them out loud with you taking one part and your friend, companion, relation, co-worker or colleague reading the other.

Enjoy!

Michael Rosen
February 2025

THEIR FAULT

'There are some people who say that the war is our fault,' said the King.

'Ridiculous,' said the tutor.

'Well, put it this way,' said the King, 'it was obvious at the beginning it was the enemy's fault but there are some people who are starting to say that what's going on now is beginning to be our fault.'

'Ridiculous,' said the tutor.

'That's what I say,' said the King, 'but they won't listen.'

'Then,' said the tutor, 'you have to make sure that you keep saying that it's their fault.'

'I do, I do,' said the King, 'but these people see pictures, tutor, and, say, for example that we're going too far.'

'These are people who hate us,' said the tutor, 'so of course they would say that.

'But, tutor,' said the King, 'they see pictures of dead women and children.'

'Yes indeed,' said the tutor, 'which only goes to show how disgusting our enemy is.'

'Really?' said the King.

'Of course,' said the tutor, 'because, you'll remember, sir, they started it.'

'What? The women and children started it?' said the King.

'No, but it's the enemy's fault they're being killed,' said the tutor.

'But we are doing it, aren't we?' said the King.

'That may well be technically correct,' said the tutor, 'but that's war.'

'What's war?' said the King.

'Women and children being killed,' said the tutor.

'I see,' said the King.

'I thought you would,' said the tutor.

STOP

'I don't think we can stop this game of chess,' said the King, 'until we decide what kind of stop it is.'

'A pause,' said the tutor.

'Or a momentary break?' said the King.

'Or a cessation of activity, perhaps,' said the tutor.

'Or a temporary halt,' said the King.

'I prefer an agreed discontinuance,' said the tutor.

'I can only go with a reasonable outage,' said the King.

'Well,' said the tutor, 'if we can't agree on what to call it, we can't stop.

'Fair enough,' said the King, 'on we go.'

SANCTITY

'Today we're talking about the sanctity of human life,' said the King's tutor.
   'Oh I like the sound of that,' said the King.
   'Exactly,' said the tutor, 'we like the sound of it.'
   'Do we like the sanctity itself, though?' said the King.
   'Only when we choose to like it,' said the tutor. 'At other times, we ignore it.'
   'You mean some human life has more sanctity than others?' said the King.
   'Yes,' said the tutor.

DEMANDS

'I should warn you, sir, that people will come to you demanding all sorts of things,' said the King's tutor.

'Like what?' said the King.

'Freedom. Food. Peace. Those sorts of things,' said the tutor.

'And I should do what I can to help them?' said the King.

'No,' said the tutor.

'What then?' said the King.

'You say that you'd like to but it's not a simple matter. In fact, it's much more complicated than they think,' said the tutor.

'I get it,' said the King, 'freedom, food and peace are much more complicated than they think.'

'Good,' said the tutor.

A MAP

'Geography today, sir,' said the King's tutor, 'I want you to draw a map.'

'What of?' said the King.

'Anywhere you like,' said the tutor, 'pick a part of the world where you would like to be King and draw the map.'

'Like this?' said the King.

'Excellent,' said the tutor.

'Now what?' said the King.

'That's it,' said the tutor, 'you've drawn it, so that's the way it is.'

IN THE WAY

'What you have to realise, sir,' said the King's tutor, 'is that some people are in the way.'

'What are they in the way of?' said the King.

'Us,' said the tutor.

'Where?' said the King.

'Not actually in the way of you, here, right now,' said the tutor, 'I mean they are in the way of your long term objectives.'

'Oh well, if that's the case, we had better do something about it,' said the King.

'Exactly,' said the tutor.

CRITICS

'There are times when we need critics,' said the King's tutor.
'I don't like critics,' said the King.
'That's a mistake,' said the tutor, 'critics can be very useful.'
'Even when they say that we are doing the wrong things?' said the King.
'Exactly that,' said the tutor, 'but only if they first declare their absolute loyalty.'
'I still don't like them because they give comfort to our enemies,' said the King.
'You're still missing the point,' said the tutor, 'critics who are loyal, help us appear to be magnanimous, wise, tolerant and kind.'
'Maybe,' said the King.
'And, anyway,' said the tutor, 'you can carry on doing the things they are complaining about.'
'How come?' said the King.
'Because, sir, it's just words,' said the tutor. 'They do words. You do actions.'
'Good point,' said the King.

HORRIBLE THINGS

'Remember it's us who are suffering, sir,' said the King's tutor.
'Why's that?' said the King.
'Because people say horrible things about us,' said the tutor.
'Yes, but what about the people we hear about who are hungry?' said the King.
'That's the point. We just hear about it,' said the tutor.
'But we should care about them, shouldn't we?' said the King.
'We can say that we care, yes, but the point is we're the ones who are in pain,' said the tutor.

LOOKING INTO IT

'Tutor, are they concerned, or are we looking into it?' said the King.

'Possibly both,' said the King's tutor.

'Are they concerned that we're looking into it?' said the King.

'Good lord no,' said the tutor, 'when we say we're looking into it, that stops them being concerned.'

'Why's that?' said the King.

'Because we're not looking into it,' said the tutor.

'One other thing, tutor,' said the King, 'are we concerned that they are concerned?'

'Of course not,' said the tutor.

'Why not?' said the King.

'Because that's what they do,' said the tutor.

'What?' said the King.

'Be concerned,' said the tutor, 'they just keep on being concerned.'

'So no need to be concerned that they're concerned,' said the King.

'Exactly,' said the tutor.

KILLING ALL THE MICE

'What are you doing, sir?' said the King's tutor.

'I'm telling the cat that he mustn't kill all the mice,' said the King, 'only the ones that he's going to eat.'

'Is he listening?' said the tutor.

'Of course,' said the King, 'and I've told him that if he doesn't stop, I won't give him any food.'

'Are you going on giving him food?' said the tutor.

'Yes,' said the King.

'And is the cat going on killing all the mice?' said the tutor.

'Yes,' said the King.

'Well that seems to suit both of you,' said the tutor, 'you tell yourself that you're doing a good thing and the cat goes on killing the mice.'

GOOD WARS

'Why's it important to remember good wars?' said the King's tutor.
'Because we won?' said the King.
'No, that's a common mistake people make,' said the tutor.
'Because we won?' said the King.
'No,' said the tutor, 'you've already said that once.'
'I give up,' said the King.
'We remember the good wars was so that we can use them as an example for why we should be waging the next war.'
'But what if we weren't entirely good during the good wars?' said the King.
'Then that's an example of why we have to do things that aren't entirely good,' said the tutor.

WAGING WAR

'Today,' said the King's tutor, 'I want you to imagine a way of waging war where there is no danger to the people waging the war.'

'How about if we had invisible soldiers?' said the King.

'Good,' said the tutor.

'What if we had magical soldiers?' said the King, 'who could make the enemy vanish.'

'Good,' said the tutor.

'I can't think of any more,' said the King.

'What about if you had flying soldiers?' said the tutor, 'they could fly over the enemy and drop things on them.'

'That's very clever,' said the King, 'but the things they dropped would end up landing on people who aren't soldiers, wouldn't they?' said the King.

'Yes, but that wouldn't matter,' said the tutor.

IN CHARGE

'We're safe where we're sitting here, right now, aren't we?' said the King.
'Of course,' said the King's tutor.
'That's good,' said the King.
'Very good,' said the tutor, 'and that's as it should be, sir, because we're in charge. People in charge have to be safe.'
'Yes,' said the King.
'Imagine for a moment,' said the tutor, 'if the people in charge weren't safe.'
'It would be terrible,' said the King, 'they would have to find other people to be in charge.
'Unimaginable,' said the tutor, 'what'll you have on your toast, sir?'
'Marmalade, please,' said the King.
'Certainly, sir,' said the tutor.

TIT FOR TAT

'We believe in tit for tat, don't we, tutor?' said the King.

'Yes,' said the King's tutor, 'that's fair.'

'What if the tit is bigger than the tat?' said the King, 'would that still be fair?'

'If we said that it was unfortunate that the tit was bigger than the tat,' said the tutor, 'then people would think it was fair.'

'Good,' said the King.

'Also, if we said that it was the tat's fault that the tit was bigger than the tat, people would think that was fair too,' said the tutor.

'And could we still say it was fair if the tit was, say, twenty times bigger than the tat?' said the King.

'I would certainly expect you to say it's fair,' said the tutor.

'And do you think me saying that, would help people see that that was fair?' said the King.

'Yes,' said the tutor.

'Good,' said the King.

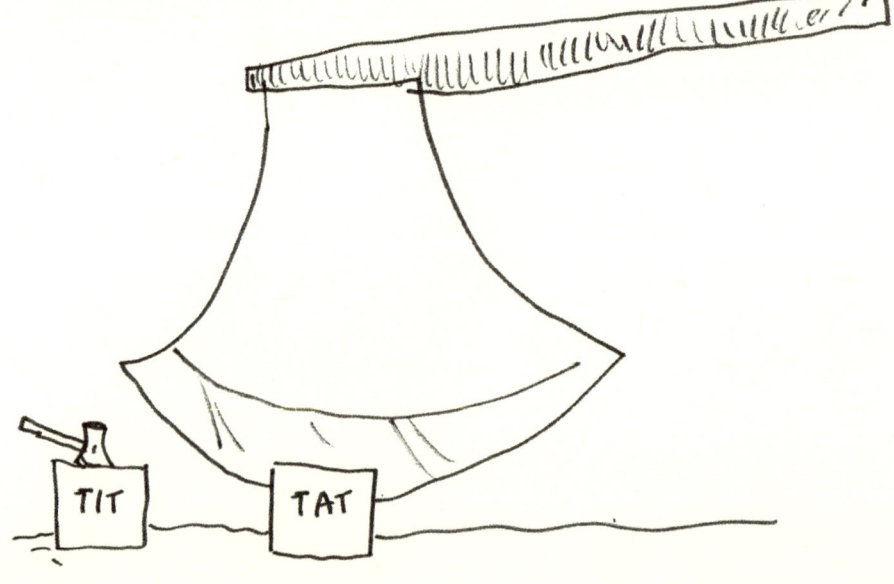

DEALING WITH IT

'We have a problem, tutor' said the King.
   'Our soldiers will deal with it,' said the King's tutor.
   'We said that last time,' said the King.
   'We did,' said the tutor.
   'And the time before,' said the King.
   'That's true,' said the tutor.
   'And the time before that,' said the King.
   'Indeed we did,' said the tutor.
   'So why are we sending the soldiers again?' said the King.
   'Because the soldiers will deal with it,' said the tutor.
   'What shall I say to the people?' said the King.
   'The soldiers are dealing with it,' said the tutor.
   'That's a good idea,' said the King.

THE ENEMY

'Say after me,' said the King's tutor, ' "The enemy is the enemy is the enemy".'

'The enemy is the enemy is the enemy,' said the King. 'Is that it?'

'Not quite,' said the tutor, 'you have to keep saying that we always defeat the enemy.'

'I don't think it's always the same kind of enemy, is it?' said the King.

'Really?' said the tutor.

'Well I remember that when the enemy was in the next door house, we knocked down the house. If the enemy lives in the same house as us, we can't just knock down the house,' said the King.

'But we can throw them out of the house,' said the tutor.

'You're always one jump ahead, aren't you?' said the King.

'Yes,' said the tutor.

BAD STUFF

'Remember this, sir,' said the King's tutor, 'there are times when you don't want them to talk about the bad stuff we do.'

'Yes,' said the King, 'how can we get that to happen?'

'We say that other stuff is worse,' said the tutor.

'Like what?' said the King.

'The fact that people hate you. That's one,' said the tutor.

'And?'

'The fact that everyone else is doing bad stuff. That's another,' said the tutor.

'This is very good,' said the King. 'Are there more?'

'The fact that the bad stuff done to us is worse than the bad stuff we're doing to them,' said the tutor.

'Is it?' said the King.

'You're missing the point, sir,' said tutor, 'this is to do with what people are talking about not whether it's true or not.'

THE PALACE

'This palace is ours, isn't it?' said the King.

'Of course it is,' said the King's tutor.

'Then why do the people living in a room upstairs think the palace is theirs?' said the King.

'Because they're wrong,' said the tutor.

'So should we at least let them have that room upstairs?' said the King.

'No,' said the tutor.

'Well how about us moving into that room upstairs?' said the King.

'Yes, we're doing that,' said the tutor, 'but there are one or two problems with that.'

'Well get the bailiffs in then,' said the King, 'and throw them out.'

'That's one of the options we're working on,' said the tutor.

FIERCELY INDEPENDENT

'We're fiercely independent, aren't we?' said the King.

'Absolutely,' said the tutor, 'and luckily the Emperor supports our independence.'

'Yes,' said the King, 'I've often wondered why he is so supportive.'

'Because we create regional stability,' said the tutor.

'Yes,' said the King, 'though I have noticed there is some occasional regional instability.'

'And when that happens the Emperor is there straightaway to help us deal with it,' the tutor.

'Could we deal with the regional instability on our own?' said the King.

'Probably not,' said the tutor.

'But we're fiercely independent, aren't we?' said the King.

'Absolutely,' said the tutor.

TITLE DEEDS

'As you keep asking me if the palace is ours, sir,' said the King's tutor, 'I've brought you the title deeds.'

'Oh very good,' said the King.

'This is where we signed the deeds,' said the tutor.

'Is that because the palace once belonged to someone else?' said the King.

'I must warn you, sir, this is very complicated,' said the tutor.

'You're right, there are a lot of signatures,' said the King, 'does that mean some of these people think the palace is theirs?'

'They think that,' said the tutor, 'it's just that they're wrong.'

'Good,' said the King, 'but how do we know they're wrong?'

'Let's flick back through all these pages, sir,' said the tutor, 'and get back to the first page.'

'Good idea,' said the King.

'What can you see?' said the tutor.

'It's signed by God,' said the King.

'Exactly,' said the tutor, 'and that's why the palace is ours.'

'That's marvellous,' said the King, 'you make everything so clear.'

SINCE

'Let's discuss the use of the word 'since',' said the King's tutor.

'Really?' said the King, 'that doesn't sound very interesting.'

'Oh but it is,' said the King's tutor. 'Let me try you with this: if I say that apples have fallen off the tree since last night's storm, what do you think?'

'Obviously, I think that the apples fell off the tree because of last night's storm,' said the King.

'Exactly,' said the tutor, 'but I didn't say 'because' of last night's storm, I said 'since', last night's storm.'

'I said this wouldn't be very interesting,' said the King.

'Wait,' said the tutor, 'what if the tree was rotten? Did the apples fall off the tree 'since' the storm or because the tree was rotten?'

'Was the tree rotten?' said the King.

'Wait, ' said the tutor, 'I have some information on the other trees.'

'Yes?' said the King.

'The apples didn't fall off the other trees,' said the tutor.

'Wow,' said the King, 'that's really interesting.'

DRASTIC MEASURES

'We have to take drastic measures, sir,' said the King's tutor.
   'Like what?' said the King.
   'I have in mind poisoning their wells,' said the King's tutor.
   'Won't they be able to smell it?' said the King.
   'No, sir,' said the tutor, 'no one will be able to detect this. It'll just happen.'
   'Good,' said the King, 'but won't it mean that everyone will be poisoned?'
   'No,' said the tutor, 'this is targeted poisoning.'
   'That's very good,' said the King, 'I have to say, tutor, you exceed yourself.'
   'Thank you, sir,' said the tutor.

HOMEWORK

'You need to learn who are our enemies and who are our enemies,' said the King's tutor.

'Mmm?' said the King, 'surely our enemies are our enemies.'

'Not so simple,' said the tutor. 'You see some of our enemies are our enemies but some of our enemies are our friends.'

'I'm not following this,' said the King.

'Well, think of it like this: those of our enemies who are not our enemies are our friends.'

'I need to do more homework on this,' said the King.

VERY MYSTERIOUS

'We're against war, aren't we, tutor?' said the King.

'We say we are,' said the King's tutor.

'So it's mysterious why we're against war but we're at war, isn't it?' said the King.

'Very mysterious,' said the tutor.

'Is anybody in favour of war?' said the King.

'Some of our scribes seem to like it,' said the tutor.

'Anyone else?' said the King.

'Yes, the people who make the swords and shields,' said the tutor, 'they're very much in favour of it.'

'Surely not,' said the King, 'because their swords and shields get damaged.'

'Surely yes,' said the tutor, 'because if they're damaged, they need to make and sell new ones.'

'Oh that's good,' said the King, 'it's very important that my people make a good living.'

REBELS

'Ah, do you remember when we were rebels, tutor?' said the King.

'Indeed I do,' said the King's tutor.

'Are we still rebels?' said the King.

'We say we are,' said the tutor.

'Right,' said the King, 'but how come there are people who rebel against us?'

'What you need to understand sir,' said the tutor, 'is that the people who say that they're rebels are not really rebels. We're the rebels, so how can they be rebels? You can't have rebels against rebels, can you? '

'That's very clear,' said the King.

MISTAKES

'Do we make mistakes, tutor?' said the King.

'I don't think you've phrased that right,' said the King's tutor.

'How do you mean?' said the King.

'You said, "do we make mistakes". The question you should ask is "were mistakes made?",' said the tutor.

'Alright then. Were mistakes made?' said the King.

'Yes,' said the tutor.

'Who by?' said the King.

'There you go again,' said the tutor, 'asking the wrong question.'

'Even so,' said the King 'I have to ask the first question, do we make mistakes?' said the King.

'No,' said the tutor.

'This isn't making any sense,' said the King.

'It's really quite simple. Mistakes were made. We are never making mistakes,' said the tutor.

'We're actually very good, then, aren't we?' said the King.

'Oh yes indeed,' said the tutor.

LIARS AND HYPOCRITES

'Sir,' said the King's tutor, 'we know that our critics are liars and hypocrites.'

'That's good,' said the King, 'but how do we know that?'

'Because it's only us they criticise,' said the tutor.

'You mean they don't criticise any of the other Kings and Queens?' said the King.

'Exactly,' said the tutor, 'even though they're much worse than you.'

'So why do they pick on me?' said the King.

'Because they don't like us,' said the tutor. 'They would pick on us and find fault with us even if we were not doing anything wrong.'

'So that proves that we aren't doing anything wrong?' said the King.

'Well I wouldn't go quite as far as that but, yes, that's why I'm making the point,' said the tutor.

'You mean, if we keep saying, 'But you're not moaning about the other Kings and Queens, people will immediately realise that we're not doing anything wrong?'

'That's what we'll say,' said the tutor.

'Yes, let's,' said the King.

A SPECIAL DAY

'Good news, sir,' said the King's tutor, 'I've heard we have 20 million people overseas who think it's wonderful we're here.'

'That's nice,' said the King.

'There are one or two issues with it,' said the tutor, 'they say that there'll come a special day – and it's coming soon – when we all have to become like them.'

'I'm very glad that they think it's wonderful we're here, but I don't want to become like them,' said the King.

'Oh but they say we have to, otherwise it won't be a special day,' said the tutor.

'Well tell them to go away,' said the King, 'we don't need 20 million people like that.'

'Well, that's not strictly true, sir,' said the tutor, 'you see the Emperor needs the 20 million and we need the Emperor.'

'Can't we come to some sort of deal with the 20 million so that they go on thinking it's wonderful we're here but we don't have to become like them?' said the King.

'No sir,' said the tutor, 'the deal is that that's what we have to do: become like them.'

'What should we do?' said the King.

'We sign the deal with them,' said the tutor.

'Will we have to become like them?' said the King.

'Of course not,' said the tutor, 'the special day is never going to happen.'

'So it's a joke?' said the King.

'In a way,' said the tutor, 'and in the meantime, we're all happy. They like it that we're here. The Emperor needs them. We need the Emperor. We all get on.'

'You see everything so clearly, don't you?' said the King.

'Yes,' said the tutor.

SWORDSMANSHIP

'Time for your swordsmanship class, sir,' said the King's tutor.

'Ready,' said the King.

'Today we're concentrating on defence,' said the tutor, 'raise your sword and run towards me with your sword pointing towards me.'

'Oh,' said the King, 'I wasn't expecting to be doing this in defence class.'

'Ah,' said the tutor, 'that's because you don't understand defence.'

'What if, when I reach you with my sword, my sword goes straight through you?' said the King.

'That would be what we experts in swordsmanship call a classic defence move,' said the tutor.

'Right,' said the King, 'I'm going to give this a try.'

SCIENCE

'Today,' said the King's tutor, 'we're going to do some science.'

'Oh good,' said the King.

'I want you to sit where you are and wait to see what happens, said the tutor.

'I can do that,' said the King.

'IT'S NOT RIGHT! IT'S NOT RIGHT! IT'S NOT RIGHT!' the tutor shouted.

'I'm sorry about that,' said the King.

'IT'S NOT RIGHT! IT'S NOT RIGHT! IT'S NOT RIGHT!' the tutor shouted.

'I'm very sorry about that,' said the King.

'That's the end of the experiment,' said the tutor.

'Really?' said the King, 'What happened?'

'While you were looking at me shouting 'IT'S NOT RIGHT', the cat ate your breakfast,' said the tutor.

PRINCIPLE

'What principle are we using?' said the King.
   'Eradication of vermin, sir,' said the King's tutor.
   'You mean as for rats, fleas, mice and the like?' said the King.
   'Exactly,' said the tutor.
   'Excellent,' said the King.
   'Glad you like it, sir,' said the tutor.
   'One thing, though, tutor,' said the King, 'do we actually eradicate vermin?'
   'No sir,' said the tutor, 'but it's the principle that matters.'
   'Yes,' said the King.

NO LONGER OUR FRIENDS

'I've heard that there are people who think badly of us,' said the King.

'Yes,' said the King's tutor, 'they are our enemies.'

'But I've heard that we have friends who also think badly of us,' said the King.

'Then they are no longer our friends,' said the tutor.

'That seems a pity,' said the King, 'don't we need all the friends we can get?'

'No,' said the tutor, 'we just need the friends that matter.'

LOVE

'Today we're going to talk about love,' said the King's tutor.

'Oh good,' said the King, 'this should be fun.'

'The first thing to remember about love, sir,' said the tutor, 'is that there's too much of it.'

'You've surprised me there,' said the King, 'I was going to say that there isn't enough of it.'

'A common error,' said the tutor, 'but you should remember that a good deal of love is what spoils things,'

'Oh dear,' said the King.

'Love, sir, leads people to work with others which in turn leads people to trust others,' said the tutor.

'Yes,' said the King, 'is that bad?'

'Of course it is,' said the tutor, 'trust ruins everything. It's only by assuming that people cannot be trusted that we can progress.'

DO AS YOU WOULD...

'Sir, do you remember the old phrase, "Do as you would be done by", said the King's tutor.

'Yes,' said the King, 'I do.'

'Well forget it,' said the tutor.

'Really?' said the King, 'I thought it was a wise thought.'

'No,' said the tutor, 'you have completely misunderstood the state of the world. You should think of what has been done to you and do unto others what others have done to you.'

'I think I prefer, "Do as you would be done by",' said the King.

'Then you will fill your mind with fantasies about how you want people to be nice to you,' said the tutor, 'and you will follow that by you trying to be nice to others.'

'Yes, that is what I had in mind,' said the King.

'Then you will bring disaster on us all,' said the tutor.

HISTORY

'I've been doing some History homework, tutor,' said the King.
'That's good,' said the King's tutor, 'which History?'
'Treaties,' said the King, 'I've been reading about treaties.'
'And?' said the tutor.
'They're very interesting,' said the King, 'people seem to have wars, then they stop and have treaties.'
'Yes,' said the tutor, 'and what do you learn from that?'
'Well,' said the King, 'perhaps people could miss out the wars and just have treaties instead?'
'Wrong conclusion,' said the tutor. 'The right conclusion is that people should miss out the treaties.'
'What? And just have wars?' said the King.
'Yes indeed,' said the tutor, 'because it's wars that sort things out.'
'Until the next war,' said the King.
'Exactly,' said the tutor.
'What if we were losing the wars?' said the King.
'No,' said the tutor, 'I'm talking about winning wars.'
'Endless winning?' said the King.
'That's it,' said the tutor.

UNWORTHY

'I fear you've been listening to wrong people again, sir,' said the King's tutor.
  'How so?' said the King.
  'You seem to think that you are King of all the people,' said the tutor.
  'Indeed I am,' said the King.
  'This is an old-fashioned Idea, sir,' said the tutor, 'and you would do well to get rid of it.'
  'What do you suggest?' said the King.
  'I suggest that you should think of some of the people as unworthy,' said the tutor.
  'Are they unworthy because of what they have done or because of who they are?' said the King.
  'They are unworthy because they are there,' said the tutor.
  'I see,' said the King, 'so how can they become worthy?' said the King.
  'By not being there,' said the tutor.

BADNESS

'Tutor,' said the King, 'how do we measure badness?'

'Badness,' said the King's tutor, 'is what others do to us.'

'But the other day, you said that we should do unto others what others do unto us,' said the King. 'That means that badness must also be what we do unto others.'

'Good point,' said the tutor, 'but you've overlooked something.'

'What?' said the King.

'The difference between what we do and what we say,' said the tutor.

'You mean,' said the King, 'we might do unto others what others do unto us but we say that we don't?'

'That's it,' said the tutor.

'And people will believe what we say?' said the King.

'Of course,' said the tutor.

BORDERS

'Geography today,' said the King's tutor.

'I remember,' said the King, 'History is chaps and Geography is maps.'

'Yes,' said the tutor, 'though we might be talking about the chaps on the maps.'

'Go on,' said the King.

'Let's think about borders,' said the tutor.

'Yes,' said the King, 'they've been around for ages, haven't they? And we should respect borders.'

'Not really,' said the tutor. 'Borders are drawn on the map by whoever wins.'

'I had no idea,' said the King.

'Let me show you,' said the tutor. 'You're sitting opposite me. Between us is a border. Now let's say that I want the border to be behind you. I'll just get up and draw the border there.'

'But now we're both on the same side of the border,' said the King.

'Yes,' said the tutor, 'and that's why I'm going to push you over that border. And now the border is between us once more.'

'And you've got the place where I was standing before,' said the King.

'As I told you,' said the tutor, 'borders are drawn by whoever wins.'

HOPE

'I woke up this morning, tutor, full of hope,' said the King.

'What a pity,' said the King's tutor.

'A pity?' said the King, 'but hope is what keeps me going.'

'You should start the day with despair,' said the tutor.

'Surely not,' said the King.

'The problem with hope,' said the tutor, 'is that you bestow others with good motives.'

'Yes,' said the King.

'You need to despair of others, in order to give yourself the motive to act for yourself,' said the tutor.

A PET

'I think it's time you got a pet,' said the King's tutor.

'What a good idea,' said the King.

'What pet would you like?' said the tutor.

'I like fluffy little animals like kittens and hamsters,' said the King.

'I recommend getting a wolf,' said the tutor.

'A wolf? A wolf would attack me and try to eat me,' said the King.

'There are ways of stopping that happening,' said the tutor.

'But people will think that I am dangerous and they will shun me,' said the King.

'Think of that as an advantage,' said the tutor.

'But even if the wolf doesn't attack me and try to eat me, how can I stop it from attacking and trying to eat other people?'

'You can't,' said the tutor, 'and you shouldn't try.'

'So where can I get this wolf?' said the King.

'I will make arrangements,' said the tutor.

AN EXPERIMENT

'Today,' said the King's tutor, 'I want to try an experiment.'
'Oh good,' said the King, 'I like experiments.'
'See that I have in my hand a watch,' said the tutor.
'Yes,' said the King, 'that's my watch.'
'You say it's your watch,' said the tutor, 'but it's in my hand.'
'Then I'll ask you to give it back to me,' said the King.
'No,' said the tutor, 'the watch is in my hand so it's mine.'
'This is silly,' said the King, 'please give me back my watch.'
'No,' said the tutor.
'Then I'm going to make you give it to me,' said the King.
'Your problem with that,' said the tutor, 'is that I'm bigger and stronger than you are.'
'I see that,' said the King, 'so I'm not going to get my watch back, am I?'
'Correct,' said the tutor, 'and I like your watch.'
'I don't like this experiment,' said the King.

FALSE FRIENDS

'Have you ever heard the expression, 'false friends', sir?' said the King's tutor.

'No,' said the King, 'what are they?'

'Can you imagine you have had a friend all your life?' said the tutor.

'Yes, I can,' said the King.

'Your friend supports you in everything you do,' said the tutor.

'Yes,' said the King.

'One day, in extreme circumstances, your friend expresses doubts about what you're doing,' said the tutor.

'Yes, I'm imagining that,' said the King.

'That is a false friend,' said the tutor.

'But maybe this friend is advising me that I've done something wrong,' said the King.

'That is not possible,' said the tutor, 'and when your friend expresses these doubts, all that he is doing is assisting your enemy.'

'Oh dear,' said the King, 'but what if the doubts that my friend expresses suggest that what I'm doing harms myself?'

'Doesn't matter,' said the tutor, 'just remember: the friend who doubts is not a friend.'

'Thanks for that,' said the King, 'by the way, are you my friend?'

'Absolutely not,' said the tutor, 'I'm your tutor and that's why I can be trusted.'

SUFFERING

'Are the people suffering?' said the King.
   'No,' said the King's tutor.
   'It's just that I heard that they are,' said the King.
   'If you heard that,' said the tutor, 'then whoever was telling you, was lying.'
   'What if they were telling the truth?' said the King.
   'Then we would say they were lying,' said the tutor.
   'But wouldn't that be lying?' said the King.
   'I don't think you need to worry yourself about that,' said the tutor.

THE PROBLEM

'For many years,' said the King's tutor, 'we've had a seemingly intractable problem.'

'Which problem is that?' said the King.

'That there are people who don't like us,' said the tutor.

'Oh yes, I remember them, why don't they like us?' said the King.

'You're asking the wrong question,' said the tutor, 'you should be asking what should we do with them?'

'Alright, what should we do with the people who don't like us?' said the King.

'We should tell them that they should leave,' said the tutor.

'That is so simple and yet so good,' said the King.

'Thank you, sir,' said the tutor.

'One thing: where should they go?' said the King.

'That's not our problem,' said the tutor.

'And if they don't go?' said the King.

'Leave that to me,' said the tutor.

WHAT NEXT?

'Tutor, have you ever been in what I might call the 'What Next? Situation',?' said the King.

'No,' said the King's tutor, 'I always know what to do next. Tell me more.'

'When I was a boy, I used to love building dams in streams,' said the King. 'I would try using sticks. And the stream kept flowing. I would try using rocks. The stream kept flowing. I tried using sticks and rocks and earth, and the stream would stop for a while, but in the end the stream kept flowing. I was in a 'What's Next? Situation'.'

'But you were a boy. The problem would have been easily solved with a cement mixer and cement,' said the tutor. 'As I said, I always know what to do next.'

'But if you did use cement, the water will build up and go over the top of the dam,' said the King, 'or round the sides.'

'Then I'll go back higher up the stream and divert it,' said the tutor. 'I always know what to do next.'

'But the stream is part of the landscape,' said the King, 'you've just changed the landscape.'

'Yes,' said the tutor, 'I always know what to do next.'

ARE OUR ENEMIES HUMAN?

'Tutor, should we sympathise with our enemies?' said the King.

'No,' said the King's tutor.

'Let me put it another way,' said the King, 'are our enemies human?'

'They are, in a biological sense,' said the tutor, 'but it doesn't help us to think of them as human.'

'Why's that?' said the King.

'Because of the terrible crimes they commit,' said the tutor.

'Do we commit terrible crimes?' said the King.

'No,' said the tutor.

'And when we say 'enemies', is that their leaders or is it everyone who the leaders lead?' said the King.

'We say it's the leaders but in the end, it's easier to think of it as being everyone,' said the tutor.

'That seems a bit harsh,' said the King.

'Needs must,' said the tutor, 'we have to think of our long-term objectives.'

'Oh yes,' said the King, 'I forgot about them.'

'That's why you've confused yourself with this talk of sympathy,' said the tutor, 'remember, sir, our enemies want to destroy us.'

'And 'enemies' means in the end, that's everyone wanting to destroy us?' said the King.

'Yes,' said the tutor.

'So, if they all want to destroy us, we have to destroy all of them?' said the King.

'Well,' said the tutor, 'we should at the very least show that that's what we are ready to do.'

'Ah like the old song, 'It ain't what you do, it's the way that you do it, and that's what get's results',' said the King.

'Exactly,' said the tutor.

'Will it get results?' said the King.

'Of course,' said the tutor.

FRIENDS

'Tutor,' said the King, 'some of our friends are expressing concerns.'
'Oh no, not again,' said the King's tutor.
'Don't you think we should listen to them?' said the King.
'We can listen to them,' said the tutor, 'but on no account do what they say.'
'But they're our friends,' said the King.
'Remember, sir, they are just what you say they are, 'friends',' said the tutor, 'that means that they're just wailing on the sidelines.'
'No,' said the King, 'they're trying to help us.'
'You've got the wrong end of the stick,' said the tutor, 'they're just trying to help themselves.'
'How's that?' said the King.
'They know that when they express concerns,' said the tutor, 'it won't have any effect on what we do, but others will hear them wailing from the sidelines, and so think that they're good people. Then they can feel better about themselves. They're helping themselves.'
'So, really it's us who are helping them feel good,' said the King.
'We do our best,' said the tutor.

NORMAL PEOPLE

'Can people who criticise us be good, normal people?' said the King.

'It's an interesting thought,' said the King's tutor, 'but my first response is, No.'

'Why's that?' said the King.

'Because it can be shown that people who criticise us have ulterior motives,' said the tutor.

'Well, we all have those, don't we?' said the King.

'Ah yes,' said the tutor, 'but these people's ulterior motives are bad.'

'All of them?' said the King. 'Don't you think it's possible that, say, one of them . . . or two of them, could be good, normal people without bad ulterior motives?'

'It's safer to say no. In other words, it's not possible,' said the tutor.

'So who are the good and normal people?' said the King.

'First and foremost, it's us,' said the tutor, 'and second, it's people who don't criticise us, and third, it's people who praise us.'

'It's good to see it laid out like that, so clearly,' said the King.

RICH

'The good thing about our country,' said the King, 'is that anyone can become rich.'

'That's true,' said the King's tutor, 'and it's important that we keep saying it.'

'One thing that I sometimes wonder,' said the King, 'is can everyone become rich?'

'No,' said the tutor.

'That's strange, isn't it?' said the King. 'Anybody can become rich but everybody can't.'

'Strange but necessary,' said the tutor.

'Do you know why or how that comes about?' said the King.

'One explanation is that not everybody is clever enough to be rich,' said the tutor, 'but the trouble with that explanation is that some rich people are not clever.'

'Yes,' said the King.

'Another explanation is that it takes a special mix of drive and inventiveness to become rich,' said the tutor, 'but then some rich people have no drive or inventiveness.'

'Yes,' said the King

'We could go on like this for days,' said the tutor, 'but at the end of the day, that's the way it is, and thank goodness it is.'

'Why do you say that?' said the King.

'Well, if everyone was rich, no one would want to work for people like us,' said the tutor.

'So it's all for the good, then,' said the King.

'Of course it is,' said the tutor.

WHAT'S NECESSARY

'Is there anything we do that is worse than the fact that people say terrible things about us?' said the King.

'No,' said the King's tutor.

'That's what I thought,' said the King, 'because people are saying awful things, aren't they?'

'Yes,' said the tutor.

'And we're doing what's right, aren't we?' said the King.

'We're doing what's necessary,' said the tutor.

'And what we're doing wouldn't be terrible, would it?' said the King.

'If it's necessary, it can't be terrible,' said the tutor.

'That's a relief,' said the King, 'and if what we're doing isn't terrible and yet people are saying terrible things about us, then what they're doing – by saying terrible things – is much worse than what we're doing?'

'I think you're getting there,' said the tutor.

'I'm really glad to have sorted it out in my mind,' said the King.

WE'VE FINISHED

'We've finished,' said the King's tutor, 'but we're carrying on.'
 'Apologies,' said the King, 'there's something I haven't understood. If we've finished, why are we carrying on?'
 'Because we haven't completely finished,' said the tutor.
 'That sounds just a bit like "not finished",' said the King.
 'You say that, sir,' said the tutor, 'because you're a defeatist.'
 'Actually,' said the King, 'I'm an optimist. I hope we'll be finished soon.'
 'Good,' said the tutor.
 'How will we know when we're completely finished?' said the King.
 'When we get back to the way we were,' said the tutor.
 'But we hadn't finished when we were the way we were,' said the King.
 'That's a good point,' said the tutor.

TO PROTECT PEOPLE

'Messenger from the Emperor has been here,' said the King's tutor.

'You didn't show him in,' said the King.

'There wasn't time, sir,' said the tutor, 'he had to move on to the next kingdom.'

'What did he want?' said the King.

'He wants you to do more to protect people,' said the tutor.

'More to protect people?,' said the King, 'we're not doing anything to protect people. How can we do more?'

'It's something we say we're doing without actually doing it,' said the tutor.

'Does anyone believe that this is what we're doing?' said the King.

'Our true allies will,' said the tutor.

'But can't people see,' said the King, 'that if we're killing people, we can't be protecting them?'

'I expect that some people can see that, sir,' said the tutor.

'Then those people might think we're not telling the truth,' said the King.

'Those people might think that, sir,' said the tutor, 'but the good news is that there's nothing they can do about it.'

'That's a relief,' said the King.

CHILDREN

'Are children our enemies?' said the King.

'Of course,' said the King's tutor, 'because though they might not actually be our enemies right now, they will grow up and become our enemies.'

'What about women?' said the King.

'The problem with women is that they have babies,' said the tutor.

'Why's that a problem?' said the King.

'The babies grow into children,' said the tutor, 'and the children grow up to be our enemies.'

'What about old women who are too old to have babies?' said the King.

'The problem with women who are too old to have babies,' said the tutor, ' is that they often look after the babies that the younger women have.'

' . . . and the babies grow up to be our enemies,' said the King.

'You're getting it,' said the tutor.

SCRIBES

'I have a pretty low opinion of scribes,' said the King's tutor.

'Do you?' said the King, 'why's that?'

'They meddle,' said the tutor, 'always poking their noses into other people's business.'

'Mind you,' said the King, 'you do a fair bit of that.'

'They also spend their time writing bad news.'

'Would it be better if they pretended it was good news?' said the King.

'What would be better,' said the tutor, 'is if there were no scribes.'

'I'm not sure that that can be arranged,' said the King.

'I'm pretty sure it can be,' said the tutor.

CHESS

'You need to learn how to play chess,' said the King's tutor.

'Must I?' said the King, 'what's so special about chess?'

'Chess is a battle played out on a board.,' said the tutor.

'I know,' said the King.

'Each piece can knock out the other side's piece,' said the tutor.

'How does it do that?' said the King.

'Well, you might be sitting on a square,' said the tutor. 'Then I come along and I replace you sitting on your square with me sitting on that square.'

'Yes, but how do you do that?' said the King.

'Just as I've described it,' said the tutor, 'one moment you're on a square, then you're not on a square. I'm on it instead.'

'What's the point of that?' said the King.

'I'm not saying it has a point,' said the tutor, 'I'm just describing it.'

'But it hasn't got anything to do with real life,' said the King.

'I wouldn't say that,' said the tutor.

A RESTRAINING INFLUENCE

'Do you think we need a restraining influence?' said the King.

'We don't,' said the King's tutor.

'So why do I hear people saying that we need a restraining influence?' said the King.

'The people who say they are a restraining influence need to say that they're a restraining influence,' said the tutor.

'Why?' said the King.

'Because saying they're a restraining influence looks good,' said the tutor.

'But we don't take any notice of the restraining influence,' said the King, 'so surely no one takes any notice when the people who say they are a restraining influence, say, "Look at us, we're a restraining influence".'

'Amazingly,' said the tutor, 'the people who say they are a restraining influence actually convince some people that they are a restraining influence.'

'But you told me,' said the King, 'that the people who say they are a restraining influence are helping us, and not restraining us.'

'Exactly,' said the tutor.

'And people know that they're helping us and not restraining us?' said the King.

'Yes,' said the tutor.

'And yet they still say that they're a restraining influence?' said the King.

'Incredible, but yes,' said the tutor.

THE RIGHT PEOPLE

'It's time we thought about swapping people around,' said the King's tutor, 'too many wrong people in the places where the right people should be.'

'What should we do?' said the King.

'Move the right people into the places where the right people should be,' said the tutor.

'It sounds like a good idea,' said the King, 'but won't the wrong people be annoyed.'

'They're always annoyed about something,' said the tutor, 'so it makes no difference if they're annoyed about this too.'

'Yes,' said the King, 'but you can't always get people to move.'

'I don't think you do it by asking them to move,' said the tutor.

'Tell me more about this tomorrow,' said the King.

TOURNAMENTS

'Do you like tournaments, sir?' said the King's tutor.

'Mostly,' said the King.

'I love them,' said the tutor.

'Why's that?' said the King.

'They never stop,' said the tutor.

'They stop when one of the knights wins,' said the King.

'Not really,' said the tutor. 'When one knight has won, there's another tournament. When one knight has won that one, there's another tournament. Then the day of the tournaments ends. Then a few months later there's another day of tournaments. And a few months later, there's another one. And on and on and on it goes. I love it,'

'Yes, they do keep on coming round,' said the King.

'That's what so great about them,' said the tutor, 'It's like one long endless battle with breaks in between.'

'And that's what you like?' said the King.

'Yes,' said the tutor.

THE EMPEROR

'The Emperor is very busy today,' said the King's tutor.

'He's always busy,' said the King, 'what's he doing now?'

'Running about,' said the tutor, 'telling everyone what to do, telling them that things are a bit tricky but everything's going to be fine in the end.'

'I've never figured out if the Emperor is the solution or the problem,' said the King.

'Best not to ask,' said the tutor, 'so long as he supports us.'

A SAFE PLACE

'This is a very safe place, isn't it, tutor?' said the King.

'Yes, sir,' said the King's tutor, 'safe, but not always safe.'

'How do you mean?' said the King.

'Well the default position on this is 'safe', but things do crop up to make aspects of it that aren't safe.'

'So it's safe in between the times it's not safe?' said the King.

'Yes,' said the tutor, 'or as I prefer to think of it, 'safe, if it wasn't for the things that make it not safe'.'

'So shouldn't we do things with the things that make it not safe?' said the King.

'Of course,' said the tutor, 'and that's what we're trying to do.'

'I don't follow this very closely,' said the King, 'how long have we been trying to do things with the things that make it not safe?'

'Quite a long time,' said the tutor.

'Do we keep doing the same things to make it safe?' said the King.

'Broadly speaking yes,' said the tutor.

'Any thoughts as to whether we should try something else to make it safe?' said the King.

'We've had those thoughts,' said the tutor, 'but we've rejected them.'

'Very good,' said the King, 'if you've thought about it, that's good. In the meantime, we should just press on with what we've always been doing.'

'That's how I see it too,' said the tutor.

IT'S GOING WELL

'It's going well, isn't it?' said the King.
　'What is?' said the King's tutor.
　'Anything that should be going well,' said the King.
　'Well, if it should be going well, it is going well,' said the tutor.
　'Things don't go badly, do they?' said the King.
　'That's complicated,' said the tutor. 'Things can have gone badly in the past. It's just that they don't go badly in the present.'
　'How mysterious,' said the King.

LETTERS

'We're getting some letters complaining about what we're doing,' said the King.
'Of course we are,' said the King's tutor, 'people like complaining about us.'
'But what should be do about them?' said the King.
'We can do any of several things,' said the tutor, 'you choose.'
'Go on then,' said the King.
'First, ignore them,' said the tutor.
'Sounds good,' said the King.
'Second attack the people complaining,' said the tutor.
'You mean tell them that they're bad people?' said the King.
'Exactly,' said the tutor.
'Third is more complicated. We explain to the world that the pain we're experiencing because of their complaints is much worse than anything people are going through because of what we're doing.'
'That's daring. But will anyone believe us?' said the King.
'Of course,' said the tutor.
'Let's do that one,' said the King.

IRONIC

'We're humane, aren't we, tutor?' said the King.

'We are,' said the King's tutor, 'and it should always be remembered that even when we are inhumane, we are inhumane in a humane way.'

'Indeed,' said the King, 'and that's what's remarkable about us, isn't it?'

'Yes,' said the tutor, 'and how ironic that this is precisely what a lot of people don't understand about us.'

'Not only ironic,' said the King, 'but also tragic.'

'This is a point that needs to be made more clearly,' said the tutor, 'that the irony is a tragic irony and the tragedy is an ironic tragedy.'

'Perhaps it's too complex for ordinary people to understand,' said the King.

'Yes,' said the tutor.

THE COUNCIL

'What should we do about our Council members who say very threatening things?' said the King.

'First, we ask ourselves, "Are they threatening us?",' said the King's tutor.

'No,' said the King.

'Then we ask ourselves, "Are these people necessary for us?",' said the tutor.

'Well it's much better that they're in the Council rather than fomenting rebellion outside,' said the King.

'Good,' said the tutor, 'and then we have to ask ourselves, "Are they useful?" '

'I don't know,' said the King.

'Put it this way,' said the tutor, 'do they say things that suggest to our enemies the kind of things that we could do or might do?'

'I think so,' said the King.

'Good. But the most useful thing of all, sir,' said the tutor, 'is that you can present yourself as the one thing that is holding back these dangerous people from inflicting terrible harm.'

'Oh i do like that,' said the King.

'It gets better,' said the tutor, 'you can look like you're the one holding them back even as you are not holding back!'

'So people will praise me for being the good one in the room!' said the King.

JUDGES

'What should we do when judges are wrong?' said the King.

'Several possibilities,' said the King's tutor. 'We can kill them.'

'Seems a bit extreme,' said the King.

'We can produce some documents to show that they are corrupt, sinful and criminal,' said the tutor.

'I like that,' said the King.

'We can try and ignore them and everything they say,' said the tutor.

'Not usually possible,' said the King.

'But if we both ignore them and prevent the people from hearing what the judges say,' said the tutor, 'that might work.'

'How would we prevent the people from hearing what the judges say?' said the King.

'We make sure that the scribes are either not in court, or that we make sure that what the scribes write, isn't published,' said the tutor.

'Very neat,' said the King.

'Thank you, sir,' said the tutor.

OUTRAGE WARS

'You have to remember, sir,' said the Kings tutor, 'is that there's 'outrage' and then there are 'outrage wars.'

'Tell me more,' said the King.

'One person starts off by expressing outrage,' said the tutor.

'Yes,' said the King.

'Then someone else says, "Aha, but you didn't express outrage about that other thing",' said the tutor. ' "Aha", says the first person, "but then you didn't express outrage about this other thing over here".'

'So they're both accusing each other of not expressing enough outrage?' said the King.

'More specific than that,' said the tutor, 'they're saying that if you're going to express outrage about something, you need permission from the people who allow you to express outrage.'

'And how do you get permission?' said the King.

'By expressing outrage about that other thing,' said the tutor.

'And if you don't?' said the King.

'You get outrage wars,' said the tutor.

'Worrying,' said the King.

GLEE

'Beware of glee,' said the King's tutor.
   'Really?' said the King.
   'We are sometimes criticised in public,' said the tutor.
   'Indeed we are,' said the King.
   'It's at that moment, you need to look out for glee,' said the tutor.
   'From whom? Who's doing this glee?' said the King.
   'Onlookers, commentators, scribes,' said the tutor.
   'And they show glee just because we're being criticised?' said the King.
   'They do' said the tutor.
   'And what should we do about this glee?' said the King.
   'See it for what it is,' said the tutor.
   'And what is it?' said the King.
   'Hatred,' said the tutor.
   'But what if the criticism is justified? And we've done something wrong?' said the King.
   'We haven't done anything wrong,' said the tutor, 'focus on the glee. The glee is worse than anything we've done.'

BOASTING

'I remember,' said the King, 'when the Emperor used to boast about military success.'

'Yes,' said the King's tutor, 'but he thinks we're in a new age now.'

'But why should that stop him boasting?' said the King

'He thinks that people like to hear about him saying that he's doing what he can to stop things spreading,' said the tutor.

'But if you want military success, don't you have to spread?' said the King.

'That's why he talks about doing what he can to stop things spreading,' said the tutor.

'That's very clever,' said the King, 'has it worked in the past?'

'I'm just reading up about that,' said the tutor.

CONTROLLING THE SITUATION

'Who's controlling the situation?' said the King.

'Good question, sir,' said the King's tutor, 'to start off with, we must assume that we are.'

'Even if we're not,' said the King.

'Yes,' said the tutor, 'because even if we're not controlling the situation, saying that we are controlling the situation convinces a lot of people. If we convince a lot of people, then we are controlling the situation'

'How about the Emperor? Is he controlling the situation?' said the King.

'He hopes that if we're controlling the situation, he's controlling the situation,' said the tutor.

'So, if we're not controlling the situation, he's not controlling the situation?' said the King.

'Yes,' said the tutor.

CONSEQUENCES

'I sometimes worry about consequences,' said the King.

'Don't,' said the King's tutor.

'Really? said the King.

'Think about it,' said the tutor, 'the moment you've worried about one consequence, that consequence has happened and another consequence is on the way.'

'Perhaps I should worry about that consequence then,' said the King.

'No point,' said the tutor, 'everything is a consequence of everything else. So really all we need to do is concentrate on the present. Is the present working?'

'Possibly,' said the King.

'I'll take that as a yes,' said the tutor.

SITUATIONS

'Are we in a new situation or an old situation, tutor?' said the King.

'We have to be very careful talking about situations, in that way,' said the King's tutor.

'Why's that?' said the King.

'Because if we say it's a new situation, we take away from ourselves a chance to read out our list of all the things our enemies have been doing for years,' said the tutor.

'And if we say it's an old situation,' said the King.

'Then we admit that whatever it is our enemies say is their problem, has been going on for years,' said the tutor.

'Tricky,' said the King, 'so best to just talk about 'the' situation, you think?'

'Yes,' said the tutor, 'and it's going well.'

'Is it?' said the King.

'I don't know,' said the tutor, 'but it's important to say that it is.'

'Of course,' said the King, 'it keeps peoples' spirits up.'

BAD PEOPLE

'We're getting rid of the bad people, sir,' said the King's tutor.

'That's good,' said the King.

'It is good,' said the tutor, 'but I should warn you that in order to get rid of the bad people, sir, sometimes we get rid of good people too.'

'Oh dear,' said the King, 'does that matter?'

'That depends,' said the tutor.

'What on?' said the King.

'It depends on who thinks it matters,' said the tutor.

'Do you think it matters?' said the King.

'No,' said the tutor.

'What about the public?' said the King.

'So long as we keep saying we're getting rid of the bad people, the public won't mind that we're also getting rid of some good people,' said the tutor.

'That's good,' said the King.

TRAITORS

'I hear that some of our most loyal followers fear that we are doing the wrong things,' said the King.

'Then they are traitors,' said the King's tutor.

'I don't think they mean to be,' said the King, 'I think they think they're helping us.'

'Then they are traitors twice over, snakes in the grass, disguising their treachery with honeyed words,' said the tutor.

'But what if, what if, what if the reason we're doing what we're doing is right but the way we're doing it is wrong?' said the King.

'No distinction can be made between the objective and the method,' said the tutor.

'Ah yes,' said the King, 'that thing you taught me a few weeks ago: ends and means.'

'Yep,' that's the one,' said the tutor.

'Even if our means are mean,' said the King.

'You're getting it,' said the tutor.

DAMAGE

'There are wicked people in our midst who do great damage to our cause,' said the King's tutor.

'Of course,' said the King.

'We must vilify them and, where necessary, do what we can to prevent their words from being heard.'

'Of course,' said the King.

'When they attack our cause, they attack us as people,' said the tutor.

'Yes, yes,' said the King, 'but one thing does concern me.'

'What's that?' said the tutor.

'What if we damage our cause more even than those who try to damage us?' said the King.

'I don't follow you,' said the tutor.

'What if our cause becomes so unpopular that it's not those wicked people damaging us but it's us ourselves?' said the King.

'I think you're having one of your stupid days today,' said the tutor, 'I can't believe you're saying this.'

THE FUTURE

'I sometimes wonder about the future,' said the King.

'Good,' said the King's tutor, 'and what do you think about it?'

'I'm not really sure that everything is going to be alright,' said the King.

'Nonsense,' said the tutor, 'the future is going to be wonderful.'

'Really?' said the King, 'how do you know?'

'Because everything we're doing now is right,' said the tutor, 'and we have the support of everybody who agrees with us that what we're doing is right.'

'I see,' said the King, 'but what if, by any chance, 'we're not getting it right?'

'The only thing stopping us getting it right,' said the tutor, 'is if people like you say or suggest that we're not getting it right.'

'So we must keep saying that we're getting it right, even if we might be just a little bit worried that we might not be getting it right?' said the King.

'Exactly,' said the tutor, 'certainty is not just about being certain. A good bit of certainty is about sounding certain even if you're not.'

'Thanks for that,' said the King.

CRIMES

'If someone commits a crime against you,' said the King, 'does that entitle you to commit a crime against them?'

'Ah, let me stop you there,' said the King's tutor, 'you've got some of your terms wrong.'

'Go on,' said the King.

'A response to a crime is not a crime,' said the tutor.

'You mean any response or all responses to a crime are not crimes?' said the King.

'Let's be clear,' said the tutor, 'someone commits a crime against you, you are entitled to respond.'

'I'm not sure that answers my question,' said the King, 'what I'm trying to find out is if you're entitled to make any kind of response?'

'Let me answer it a different way,' said the tutor. 'If someone commits a crime against you, you must say that your response is not a crime.'

'But what if my response was criminal,' said the King.

'What you need to understand,' said the tutor, is that that's not possible. It's not possible for our response to be criminal.'

'That's good to know,' said the King.

MOST PEOPLE DON'T UNDERSTAND

'Do people know what's going on?' said the King.

'Yes and no,' said the King's tutor, 'why do you ask?'

'Mostly because I don't know what's going on,' said the King, 'so I thought if I don't know what's going on then maybe other people don't know what's going on.'

'Do you think that matters?' said the tutor.

'Yes," said the King, 'people should know, shouldn't they?'

'Yes and no,' said the tutor.

'How do you mean?' said the King.

'Well, we can't have everyone knowing everything,' said the tutor.

'No?' said the King.

'No,' said the tutor.

'Why not?' said the King.

'Because most people don't understand what they know,' said the tutor.

'Of course not,' said the King.

'So we tell them what they need to understand,' said the tutor.

'You tell them what they need to understand before they know what's going on, then,' said the King.

'Exactly,' said the tutor.

'That's all good then,' said the King.

'Indeed,' said the tutor.

HOW WILL IT END?

'Tutor,' said the King, 'how do you think it will end?'
　'What a strange question,' said the King's tutor.
　'We need to have some idea about how it will end,' said the King.
　'That's where you're wrong,' said the tutor.
　'You surprise me,' said the King.
　'We don't need to have any ideas about how it will end,' said the tutor, 'all we need to know is if it's going well now.'
　'I see,' said the King, 'and is it?'
　'Of course,' said the tutor.
　'So can I ask instead, do you think it will end well?' said the King.
　'All we need to know is that if it's going well, it'll end well,' said the tutor.
　'Yes,' said the King, 'I just wonder a bit if that really is all we need to know.'

THE SOLUTION

'Our friends abroad are committed to a solution,' said the King.
    'We're not,' said the King's tutor.
    'Oh dear,' said the King, 'what should we do?'
    'Carry on,' said the tutor.
    'But what will be the solution?' said the King.
    'The solution that comes from carrying on,' said the tutor.
    'But what if the solution turns out not to be a solution?' said the King.
    'Doesn't matter,' said the tutor, 'because we'll just carry on.'
    'Might they complain that we're carrying on?' said the King.
    'Oh yes,' said the tutor, 'they always complain that we're carrying on but the good thing is that they never do anything about it.'
    'All good then,' said the King.

PUNISHING PEOPLE

'Tutor,' said the King, 'do you think we can punish people for crimes that they haven't yet committed?

'Yes,' said the King's tutor.

'I think there are risks in doing that,' said the King, 'we might end up punishing people who were never going to commit a crime.'

'I don't think that matters,' said the tutor, 'because of the effect it has on those who would go on and commit a crime.'

'What effect would that be?' said the King.

'It'll put them off committing a crime,' said the tutor.

'But there are a lot of people committing crimes,' said the King, 'it doesn't seem to be working.'

'But just think how many more it would be, if we didn't punish people who haven't committed crimes,' said the tutor.

'Yes,' said the King, 'good point. So we should just go on punishing people whether they've committed a crime or not.'

'Yes,' said the tutor.

MODERN TIMES

'The good thing about modern times,' said the King to his tutor, 'is that powerful people can't get away with wiping out a whole population.'

'That's exactly what we say,' said the tutor.

'Oh!' said the King, 'when you said that, you made it sound as if it's something we 'say' but not really believe.'

'Well, let's be reasonable about this, sir,' said the tutor, 'as I've often explained to you: there's always a difference between what we say and what we do.'

'Yes,' said the King, 'so how does that apply to what I'm saying today?'

'Well,' said the tutor, 'you're absolutely right about how ridiculous it would be if we announced, "We're wiping out a whole people" and then even more ridiculous, if we then went ahead and did it.'

'Exactly,' said the King, 'my very point.'

'Ah but that's where you haven't quite twigged what I'm on about,' said the tutor.

'No I haven't,' said the King.

'You see,' said the tutor, 'let's imagine a circumstance where it was indeed necessary to wipe out a whole population.'

'Right,' said the King.

'And, as you say, we can't "get away" with announcing that or doing it in one fell swoop,' said the tutor.

'Yes, I'm following this,' said the King.

'So how do we do it?' said the tutor, 'how would we have to do it?'

'No, I don't know,' said the King.

'In slices,' said the tutor, 'bit by bit. Some here. Some there.'

'But people will notice,' said the King.

'Yes,' said the tutor, 'but they'll only notice the slices. The small numbers.'

'But the people who are left standing will add up the numbers and tell everyone,' said the King.

'And we'll tell everyone not to believe the numbers,' said the tutor.

'Oh my, oh my,' said the King, 'I hadn't thought of that. "We'll tell everyone not to believe the numbers". That is so clever.'

'Thank you, sir,' said the tutor.

'No, thank YOU,' said the King.

PAIN

'What do you think about pain?' said the King to his tutor.

'Whose pain?' said the tutor.

'Pain,' said the King, 'just pain.'

'No, sir,' said the tutor, 'you're not looking at this matter in the right way. You see, there is our pain and their pain.'

'I don't follow you,' said the King.

'Our pain is important,' said the tutor.

'Of course it is,' said the King, 'but what about their pain?'

'That's where it gets complicated,' said the tutor.

'Go on,' said the King.

'You see, at one level their pain is also important,' said the tutor, 'but at another level it isn't.'

'I don't understand,' said the King.

'Well, at a very basic level, their pain must be the same as our pain,' said the tutor, 'but the question arises as to whether their pain matters as much as our pain.'

'I thought you said their pain is important,' said the King.

'Well,' said the tutor, 'it can be important but as far as you and I are concerned, it might also not matter.'

'That sounds very interesting,' said the King.

'Yes, and if we take it to its logical conclusion,' said the tutor, 'if their pain doesn't matter to us, it's our job to make that clear to everyone else.'

'How do we do that?' said the King.

'The simplest and most effective way,' said the tutor, 'is to make clear that their pain is their fault.'

'Very good,' said the King.

'And the other way,' said the tutor, 'is to make clear that they are not really, in the final analysis, the same kind of people as us.'

'How do you mean?' said the King, 'you mean not as essentially good like us?'

'Yes,' said the tutor.
''And this works?' said the King.
'Mostly,' said the tutor.
'Thanks goodness for that,' said the King.

NEGOTIATIONS

'Let's have a talk about negotiations,' said the King to his tutor.

'That's a good idea,' said the King's tutor.

'I don't really get why we bother,' said the King.

'Neither do I,' said the tutor.

'Then why do we do them?' said the King.

'Well,' said the tutor, 'mostly because everyone out there says that we should.'

'That's really boring, isn't it?' said the King.

'Yes,' said the tutor.

'Hmm,' said the King, 'so given that we have to do them, what do we do?'

'We say that we are willing to negotiate,' said the tutor.

'Even though we're not willing,' said the King, 'Then what?'

'We faff about,' said the tutor.

'Oh is that where you wave bits of paper about?' said the King.

'Exactly,' said the tutor.

'Then what?' said the King.

'I give you proof that the other side wrecked the negotiations last time and you tell everyone about that,' said the tutor.

'Why do I do that?' said the King.

'To show the world that we are willing negotiators and the other side are not, and never are,' said the tutor.

'Good,' said the King, 'then what?'

'At some point, once the negotiations get going, I tell you that the negotiations have broken down. I give you a reason. I say that they have broken down because, as we predicted, the other side have made impossible demands,' said the tutor.

'But will they have made impossible demands?' said the King.

'That's neither here nor there,' said the tutor, 'the point is the negotiations break down and we say that it's the other side's fault.'

'Then what?' said the King.
'We carry on,' said the tutor.
'Which is what we wanted to do in the first place,' said the King.
'You've worked hard in today's lesson,' said the tutor, 'well done.'

TRUTH

'What's your view on truth, tutor?' said the King to his tutor.

'Why do you ask?' said the King's tutor.

'I'm thinking about how it is that people get to know about the truth,' said the tutor.

'Interesting,' said the King, 'because it all depends on what the people first hear. Let's suppose, that the people hear that my foresters cut a tree down.'

'In that case,' said the tutor, 'you must ask yourself, 'Do I want the people to believe my foresters cut the tree down or not?''

'Let's say, that I don't want them to believe that my foresters cut down the tree,' said the King, 'what next?'

'On your behalf, I issue a statement saying that there is no truth whatsoever in the suggestion that the King's foresters cut down the tree,' said the tutor.

'But people will know that my foresters cut down the tree,' said the King.

'Ah, that's where you oversimplify things,' said the tutor, 'you see, when we say that there is no truth whatsoever in the suggestion that the King's foresters cut down the tree, it causes confusion. The people who thought that we cut down the tree are now not so certain. Next time they speak about the tree, they will say things like, 'we had understood that the King's foresters cut down the tree, but on the other hand, the King says there is no truth in this'. Did you hear that 'on the other hand' bit?'

'Yes I did,' said the King, 'and now I don't know myself whether my foresters cut down the tree!'

'Very funny, sir,' said the tutor, 'because after all, it was just a story you made up!'

'Yes indeed, just a story,' said the King, 'just a story . . .'

DIVIDED

'Does it matter that our government council has shrunk? said the King to his tutor.

'Absolutely not,' said the King's tutor.

'But people are saying that it looks bad,' said the King, 'and it shows that we are divided amongst ourselves.'

'Nonsense,' said the tutor, 'it shows precisely the opposite. We are now a leaner, more efficient government council and therefore we can get on with the job more speedily.'

'I'm concerned that those who are no longer in the government council will criticise us from outside,' said the King.

'That's good,' said the tutor 'it shows that we are tolerant.'

'I can't help thinking that there's fewer and fewer of us left,' said the King.

'Also good,' said the tutor, 'better the strong few than the divided many.'

'You're very good at these slogans, aren't you, tutor,' said the King.

'I like to think so,' said the tutor.

'But are we going to win?' said the King.

'As long as you and I are here in the palace,' said the tutor, 'we're winning.'

'Good,' said the King.

ATROCITIES

'They say we're committing atrocities,' said the King to his tutor, 'how should we reply?'

'There are several possibilities,' said the tutor, 'and we should consider any or all of them, depending on who's saying that about us.'

'Go on,' said the King.

'We can say, "No, we're not",' said the tutor.

'Yes,' said the King, 'straight denial. Does that work?'

'It gives our followers hope and courage,' said the tutor.

'I see,' said the King. 'Any others?'

'We can say, "We're doing all we can to prevent such things happening",' said the tutor.

'Are we?' said the King.

'That's besides the point,' said the tutor, 'the important thing is to say it. Please try to keep up.'

'Yes, of course,' said the King, 'anymore?'

' "Other people did stuff like this",' said the tutor.

'Do we have to say who these other people are?' said the King.

'Ideally, you should pick on a heroic conflict where the winners were justified and right,' said the tutor.

'But what if some nit-picking historian comes along and says that even though that war was justified and right, they or we committed atrocities?' said the King.

'That's a good point but no one will hear the nit-picking historian. They will just hear that it's what had to be done in the heroic, justified and right war,' said the tutor.

'You're very good at this, aren't you?' said the King.

'I like to think so,' said the tutor.

'Any more?' said the King.

' "It's not an atrocity",' said the tutor.

'Oh, but won't people argue that it is?' said the King.

'Ahah, but that's the point,' said the tutor.

'Mmm?' said the King.

'They'll spend hours and hours and hours arguing over whether it was or was not an atrocity,' said the tutor. 'They'll have inquiries and trials. There'll be hour and hours of TV programmes and radio shows arguing over whether it's an atrocity.'

'That's bad for us though,' said the King.

'Sir, please listen,' said the tutor. 'Don't you get it? They'll be arguing over whether the word 'atrocity' is the right word to use and not over whether something bad has happened. This is all good.'

'I'm not comfortable with this,' said the King.

'Just ask yourself this: do their arguments about the meaning of the word 'atrocity' stop us doing what we're doing?' said the tutor.

'No, I suppose not,' said the King.

'There's your answer,' said the tutor.

'Thank you,' said the King, 'on we go.'

'Exactly,' said the tutor.

WE DON'T KNOW . . .

'We don't know what's going on, do we, sir?' said the King's tutor.
'Oh I think we do,' said the King.
'You missed my wink,' said the tutor, 'I was winking when I said that.'
'I don't get you,' said the King.
'We know what's going on but we don't show that we know what's going on,' said the tutor.
'What do we do when people say, 'Look what you're doing!', said the King.
'We say that the people saying such things hate us,' said the tutor.
'So even if what they are saying could just possibly be right, it can't really be right because they hate us?' said the King.
'That's it,' said the tutor.

SUCCESSFUL

'Are we successful?' said the King.

'We soon will be,' said the King's tutor.

'How soon?' said the King.

'Difficult to say,' said the tutor.

'And how will you know when we are successful?' said the King.

'When we've solved the problem,' said the tutor.

'But what if solving the problem causes another problem?' said the King.

'We'll solve that problem,' said the tutor.

'You don't think that the way we're solving problems always causes more problems?' said the King.

'Of course not,' said the tutor.

AGENDA

'Agenda for today's meeting,' said the King's tutor, 'One: what we're doing. Two: people being horrible to us.'

'Right,' said the King, 'what we're doing. What have you got to report on that?'

'No sir,' said the tutor, 'we need to talk about people being horrible to us.'

'Oh,' said the King, 'I thought you said that 'People being horrible to us' is number two on the agenda.'

'It is,' said the tutor, 'but it's the number one thing that we need to talk about.'

'Right,' said the King, 'People being horrible to us. What have you got to report on that?'

'People are being horrible to us, sir,' said the tutor.

'That's awful,' said the King.

'Yes, it is,' said the tutor, 'I've minuted that and will make sure that our scribes inform everyone of what you've just said. Thank you, sir.'

'Good,' said the King, 'now let's move on to 'what we're doing.'

'I'm afraid we've run out of time, sir,' said the tutor, 'that'll have to wait till the next meeting.'

'Oh, right,' said the King.

'I think you'll agree, sir,' said the tutor, 'it's been a very successful meeting.'

'Yes,' said the King.

HAVE I GOT THIS RIGHT?

'Have I got this right, tutor?' said the King, 'people who are not with us, are against us?'

'It's worse than that, sir,' said the King's tutor.

'Oh really? Go on,' said the King.

'People who are not with us are siding with the worst people in the world,' said the tutor.

'Oh dear,' said the King, 'that's awful.'

'In effect, simply by not being with us, they are supporting the worst people in the world. They might just as well be the worst people in the world,' said the tutor.

'Yes,' said the King, 'truly appalling. Does this mean that if people criticise what we're doing, they are in effect being the worst people in the world?'

'That's exactly it,' said the tutor.

GRAVE CONCERNS

'People are expressing grave concerns about what we're going to do next,' said the King.

'So?' said the King's tutor.

'Surely we can't have people thinking we shouldn't be doing what we're doing,' said the King.

'I think we can,' said the tutor. 'I'm disappointed that when things get tough, you turn out to be weak and feeble.'

'I just worry that we might not be doing the right thing,' said the King.

'I just worry that you don't listen to me,' said the tutor.

'I'm listening,' said the King.

'First – tell people that what we're doing is right and necessary,' said the tutor.

'Got it,' said the King.

'Second – tell the people that the worst of all things going on at the moment is that people are saying horrible things about us,' said the tutor.

'Got it,' said the King.

'That's it,' said the tutor.

'Got it,' said the King.

DEEPLY CONCERNED

'People are deeply concerned,' said the King, 'are you worried?'

'Of course, not,' said the King's tutor.

'Why not?' said the King.

'Because it means that they won't do anything,' said the tutor.

'I'm not sure you're right about that,' said the King, 'I've seen their brows furrowed with deep concern.'

'Yes,' said the tutor, 'that proves that they won't do anything.'

'I really think you've got it wrong this time,' said the King.

'What you don't understand,' said the tutor, is that they say they're deeply concerned in order to show the world that they care. They think that showing that they're deeply concerned will make them popular.'

'Does it work?' said the King.

'Probably, but even if it doesn't,' said the tutor, 'it means that we can carry on doing what we want to do, because no one is going to stop us.'

'That's good then,' said the King.

'Yes,' said the tutor.

ANCESTRAL LANDS

'You must always remember your ancestral lands, sir,' said the King's tutor.

'Oh I do, tutor,' said the King, 'but where exactly are they?'

'A good guide on that matter,' said the tutor, 'is to say that our ancestral lands are where we say they are.'

'Yes, of course,' said the King, 'though I found myself wondering when I woke up this morning, whether everyone has ancestral lands.'

'Well, there are ancestral lands and ancestral lands,' said the tutor.

'I don't follow you,' said the King.

'Some ancestral lands count and some don't,' said the tutor.

'Oh that doesn't sound very fair,' said the King.

'I don't think you need to worry your head about that, sir,' said the tutor, 'all that matters is that we've got our ancestral lands.'

'Apart from the ancestral lands we haven't got yet,' said the King,

'Good point, sir,' said the tutor, 'yes, we really need to do a lot more to get hold of them.'

'Yes,' said the King, 'I would like that . . . and you don't see any problems with that, though?'

'There would be problems,' said the tutor, 'if the Emperor thought it was a bad idea.'

'And does he?' said the King.

'Precisely the opposite,' said the tutor, 'he thinks it's a great idea.'

'Well that's all sorted then,' said the King, 'what a lovely start to the day.'

WHEN DOES HISTORY BEGIN?

'Tutor,' said the King to his tutor, 'when does history begin?'

'Good question,' said the tutor, 'and the answer is that it begins when we say it begins.'

'Really?' said the King, 'surely there are more objective ways of deciding this.'

'There may be,' said the tutor, 'but we have to think about what we want people to believe.'

'We do,' said the King.

'I mean,' said the tutor, 'people are often keen to dig up all sorts of old grievances going way, way back. That doesn't do anyone any good to go over all that.'

'Yes,' said the King, 'it's quite unpleasant the way they do that.'

'So what we do, instead,' said the tutor, 'is pick a day and state clearly, "This is when it all began".'

'I can see a problem with that,' said the King, 'it'll be only us saying that.'

'I don't think you need worry about that, 'said the tutor, 'once we've named the day, we'll find that all the scribes will write it in their Annals.'

'But I've heard that there are rebel scribes who dig up stuff that shows that the sort of thing that went on on the day that we've chosen as the first day of history, also went on before that day,' said the King, 'and what's more, say these rebel scribes, at those times, it was our side doing it,' said the King.

'That's such a tedious, pernickety point,' said the tutor, 'you can rest assured that everyone will ignore it.'

'That's good,' said the King.

'It is,' said the tutor.

HOW TO LOOK AWAY

'It's marvellous that we have many noble and distinguished visitors, is it not, tutor?' said the King to his tutor.

'It is, sir,' said the tutor, 'and we do our best to train them.'

'Do you?' said the King, 'I had no idea. What do you train them to do?'

'The first and most important thing is 'How to look away',' said the tutor.

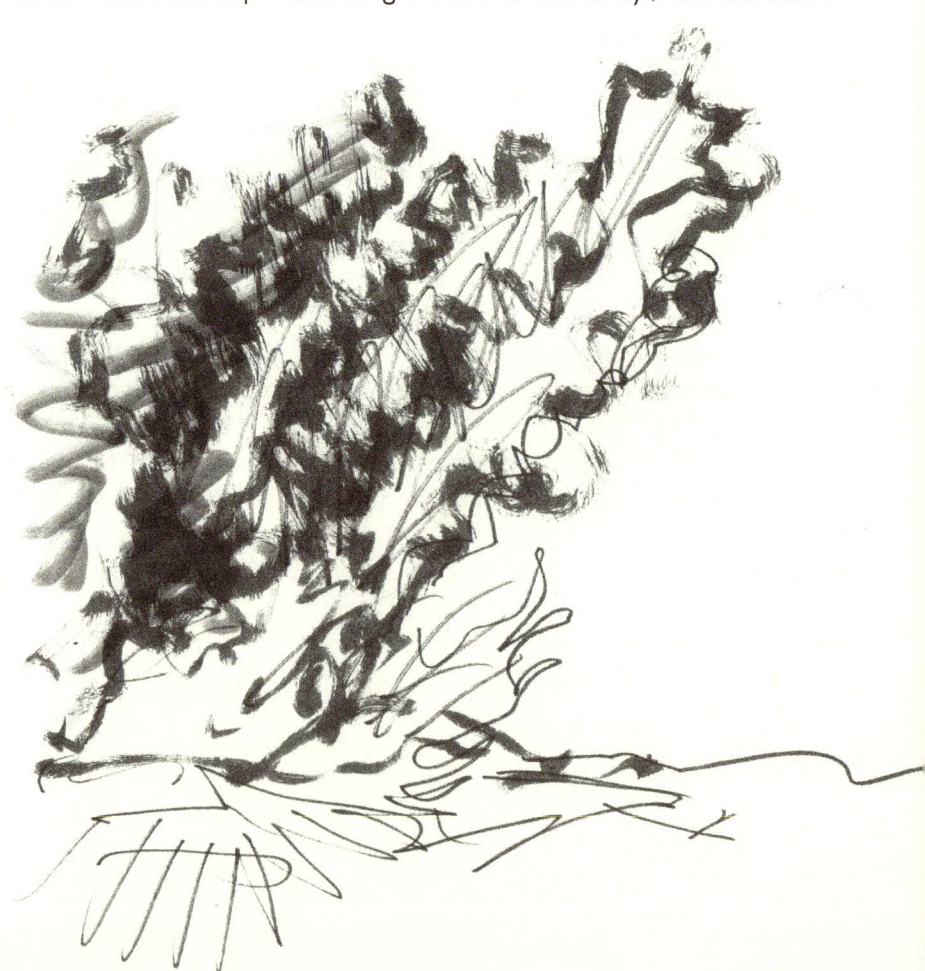

'That sounds interesting,' said the King, 'how do you do that?'

'Well sir,' said the tutor, 'we take them into a field, and explode things.'

'Do you?' said the King, 'how does that train them?'

'What happens,' said the tutor, 'is that many of them look in the direction of where the explosion happened.'

'And so they should,' said the King.

'And so they shouldn't,' said the tutor.

'But we want our visitors and their scribes to be alert, don't we?' said the King.

'No sir,' said the tutor, 'we don't. Looking in the direction of explosions is precisely the kind of thing we don't want.'

'What do we want?' said the King.

'We want them to ignore the explosions,' said the tutor.

'And how do you do that?' said the King.

'We train the visitors in how to look away,' said the tutor, 'so when one of the explosions happen, we are standing on the other side of the field, waving.'

'And then?' said the King.

'They look at us, instead of looking in the direction of where the explosions happened,' said the tutor.

'How ingenious,' said the King, 'but . . . but where does that get us?'

'People end up not asking questions about the explosions,' said the tutor.

'And that's good, is it?' said the King.

'That's very good,' said the tutor.

'I'll take your word for it,' said the King.

'I thought you would,' said the tutor.

THE KING OVER-THERE

'Some kings in other countries are terrible, aren't they Tutor?' said the King.

'Yes, indeed,' said the King's tutor.

'Do you think we should do anything about them?' said the King.

'It depends,' said the tutor, 'we start by doing deals with them.'

'But won't people say that we're unprincipled for doing that?' said the King.

'Of course,' said the tutor, 'but we say we are realists.'

'Then what?' said the King.

'Well depending on things like…the balance of power, what the Emperor says we should do, the flow of necessary goods from the area and…er…the weather, we become very concerned about the terrible King Over-There,' said the tutor.

'Yes, very concerned,' said the King, 'that's when we frown, isn't it?'

'Yes,' said the tutor, 'and then at some point, as the King Over-There is terrible, he'll do something terrible.'

'But wasn't he doing something terrible before?' said the King.

'Yes,' said the tutor, 'but that was when we were doing deals with him.'

'So now what?' said the King.

'Now we tell the world that the terrible King Over-There has been doing terrible things,' said the tutor.

'Good,' said the King, 'then what?'

'We send armies to kill the people,' said the tutor.

'The people? But won't people say that that is terrible?' said the King,

'Of course,' said the tutor, 'but we will say that that is regrettable but that it's the only way that we can get rid of the terrible King Over-There.'

'And people will believe this?' said the King,

'Some will. Some won't,' said the tutor.

'Will that matter?' said the King.

'Ah that depends on whether the people think you're terrible too,' said the tutor.

SOMETHING MONSTROUS

'People are saying that something monstrous is going on,' said the King.

'They're wrong,' said the King's tutor.

'Should we just say what you just said, then?' said the King.

'Yes,' said the tutor, 'just say that they're wrong and that it's not monstrous.'

'Anything else?' said the King,

'Tell them that they are horrible, despicable people for saying that it's monstrous,' said the tutor.

'Got that,' said the King, 'but what if it turns out that people don't believe me?'

'Are these the same people who say that something monstrous is going on?' said the tutor.

'Yes but some other people are saying it too,' said the King.

'Then they are horrible, despicable people too,' said the tutor.

'We're on the right track, then?' said the King.

'Totally,' said the tutor.

'That's good,' said the King.

NOTHING

'Tutor,' said the King, 'do you think it's possible to create nothing?'

'Good question,' said the tutor, 'I think it's theoretically possible but in reality not possible.'

'Yes,' said the King, 'that's what I thought, but are there times when we should try to create nothing?'

'Indeed,' said the tutor, 'it can be an objective.'

'Interesting,' said the King, 'you mean that on occasions, it might be worth trying to create nothing even though we know that it's not possible?'

'Yes,' said the tutor, 'the process of trying to create nothing will help us achieve our objectives.'

'That's good,' said the King.

FLAT

'Tutor,' said the King, 'can anything be completely and totally flat?'

'No,' said the Tutor, 'but it's possible to make something as flat as it can be.'

'That's an interesting way to look at it,' said the King, 'and yet we do say things like 'as flat as a pancake'.'

'Yes,' said the tutor, 'that is odd, especially as a pancake, even to the naked eye, is not really flat. Not as flat as a kitchen top, for example.'

'But we do try to make things flat, don't we?' said the King.

'Yes,' said the tutor, 'there is something pleasing to the eye about flat things, so we should regard the ambition to make things flat, a noble mission.'

'That's a very fine thought,' said the King.

OBJECTIVES

'Do you ever wonder, tutor, 'said the King, 'that we only exist because others want us to exist?'

'That's a very deep question,' said the tutor, 'I'm glad that you're thinking along philosophical lines. Go on.'

'What if,' said the King, 'we are only who we are, me the King, you the tutor, are only here because others want us to be here?'

'That would be to deny our self-will, though,' said the tutor.

'Yes, indeed,' said the King, 'but what if we are pursuing the objectives of others?'

'Too easy to say,' said the tutor, 'better that it should be expressed as two mutually approving objectives perhaps.'

'You mean it just so happens that our objectives coincide with others' objectives?' said the King.

'Yes,' said the tutor.

'The only problem with that,' said the King, 'is that I can't help feeling sometimes that we are very, very small and those who want us to be here are huge. Massive. Gigantic.'

'That's not a problem,' said the tutor, 'it's an advantage.'

CROCODILES

'Time for your lesson in ancient literature, sir,' said the King's tutor.
'Oh really?' said the King.
'Yes,' said the tutor, 'do you know the story about the crocodiles?'
'Possibly,' said the King.
'The ancients noticed that crocodiles lay in the sun and then ate people,' said the tutor.
'Of course,' said the King.
'Ah but then they noticed that the crocodiles wept,' said the tutor.
'Yes, I had heard that,' said the King.
'What do we learn from this?' said the tutor.
'That crocodiles are kind and decent creatures?' said the King.
'We learn,' said the tutor, 'that it's possible to cry about the people killed by our own actions.'
'But that would be hypocritical,' said the King.
'Perhaps,' said the tutor, 'but some people believe in the tears and think that that person is doing something to stop the killing. '
'You mean some people would go so far as to put on a false show of crying?' said the King.
'It's possible,' said the tutor.
'I can't think of anyone doing such a thing,' said the King.

HARDLY ANYONE WILL NOTICE

'Tutor,' said the King, 'I'm getting reports that people are dying.'
'Are they our people?' said the tutor.
'Not the most recent ones,' said the King, 'that was earlier.'
'Then why are you telling me?' said the tutor.
'I just thought I ought to tell you,' said the King.
'I'll ask you again sir – are they our people?' said the tutor.
'No,' said the King.
'Then that's all we need to know,' said the tutor.
'What do you mean?' said the King.
'If they're not our people, hardly anyone will notice,' said the tutor.
'But that's not to say that people are not dying, surely,' said the King.
'Well, if hardly anyone is noticing or if the only people who notice are people who don't matter, then that's all there is to it,' said the tutor.
'But there are people who matter who are noticing,' said the King.
'Are they doing anything about it?' said the tutor.
'No,' said the King.
'Then it doesn't matter,' said the tutor.
'I see,' said the King.

THE THING ABOUT WAR

'The thing about war,' said the King, 'is that it's terrible, isn't it?'

'Not necessarily,' said the tutor.

'How so?' said the King.

'Well, firstly we must remember the theory of the Just War,' said the tutor.

'Oh? What's that?' said the King.

'That's the theory that it's just a war,' said the tutor.

'I see,' said the King.

'Then there's the theory of the Clean War,' said the tutor, 'that's where everything is done cleanly.'

'Does that ever happen?' said the King.

'Oh certainly,' said the tutor, 'it's when the war is as clean as can be expected.'

'And how clean is that?' said the King.

'Try not to bother yourself with details,' said the tutor, 'it's very easy to get bogged down with numbers.'

'So maybe war isn't as terrible as people make out,' said the King.

'Ah, there's a point you need to understand, here, sir,' said the tutor, 'it all depends which war we're talking about.'

'Go on,' said the King.

'Well, let's keep it simple,' said the tutor, 'The wars we wage are just and clean. The wars that other people wage are, as you say, terrible.'

'You always make things so clear, don't you?' said the King.

'I try, sir, I try,' said the tutor.

NUTRITION

'We're going to look at nutrition today, sir,' said the King's tutor.

'Oh, isn't that just a posh word for 'eating'?' said the King.

'You should try not to be cynical,' said the tutor.

'Right then fire away,' said the King.

'The basic rule of nutrition,' said the tutor, 'is that some people need a lot of food, some people need a little and some none at all.'

'Fascinating,' said the King, 'is that voluntary?'

'How do you mean?' said the tutor.

'Do people volunteer to have a lot, a little or none?' said the King.

'Not exactly,' said the tutor, 'it's more that we create the circumstances in which these different kinds of eating take place.'

'That sounds very clever,' said the King, 'do the arrangements take up a lot of resources to implement? Does it cost a lot of money to carry out?'

'That depends,' said the tutor.

'Oh well, I'm sure it works out very well in the end,' said the King.

BEING BAD

'I'm bothered about what we should say, when people accuse us of being bad,' said the King.

'There are several things we do,' said the King's tutor.

'Oh good,' said the King, 'I thought you would know what to do.'

'First, if people say we're bad, we say that they're terrible. That neutralises anything they say about us.'

'How so?' said the King.

'Terrible people can't be right,' said the tutor.

'Good,' said the King.

'Then we say that they're picking on us – look at all the other bad people, why didn't you say that they're bad?'

'What if they did say the other bad people are bad too, though?,' said the King.

'It doesn't matter,' said the tutor, 'people will have forgotten that they said that.'

'Anything else?' said the King.

'We say that everything they say about us is lies,' said the tutor.

'Of course,' said the King, 'but what if some of it isn't lies?'

'Keep it simple, sir,' said the tutor, 'it's lies.'

'Right,' said the King.

DAY ONE

'I think we're doing well,' said the King's tutor to the King.

'How so?' said the King.

'The scribes are talking about Day One,' said the tutor.

'That's good?' said the King.

'Yes indeed sir,' said the tutor, 'because if they're talking about Day One, they're not talking about any days before Day One.'

'I'm not sure that I'm following you on this,' said the King.

'Look, if everyone's talking about Day One,' said the tutor, 'then it means people are 'getting' it that it's more important than other days.'

'But are there any days that are more important than Day One?' said the King.

'I don't think so,' said the tutor, 'but the problem is that our enemies think that there are more important days than Day One.'

'So it's kind of Battle of Days going on?' said the King.

'In a way, yes,' said the tutor, 'but we don't say that.'

'Why not?' said the King.

'Because that would be admitting that there are other days,' said the tutor.

'What went on on these other days?' said the King.

'That's precisely the kind of question we're trying to avoid, sir,' said the tutor.

'Sorry,' said the King.

'Apology accepted,' said the tutor.

PEOPLE

'Is it possible for people to not exist?' said the King to his tutor.

'Yes, of course,' said the King's tutor.

'But then, if they are people, they do exist, don't they?' said the King.

'Ah well, they may exist as persons,' said the tutor, 'but do they exist as a people?'

'I'm getting muddled, here,' said the King, 'I mean if, let's say, a few thousand persons, see things in similar ways, and see themselves in similar ways, aren't they a people?'

'Not if we don't want to call them a people?' said the tutor.

'It's down to us, is it?' said the King.

'Of course it is,' said the tutor, 'we can't leave it to the people themselves.'

'Hang on, tutor,' said the King, 'you've just called them "the people".'

'Yes,' said the tutor, 'I called them "the people", but I didn't call them "a people".'

'I really don't see the difference,' said the King.

'Then I really must help you understand,' said the tutor. 'If we sit here talking of a bunch of people as "a people", the next thing we know is that they would start claiming things to do with their people's land, or their people's right to be here.'

'Is that bad?' said the King.

'Of course it is,' said the tutor, 'we want the land for us.'

'So what can we do about these people saying that they are "a people"?'

'We keep repeating that they are not "a people", we say that they never were "a people" and that there never was anywhere where they were "a people",' said the tutor.

'Will that work?' said the King.

'It helps,' said the tutor.

'Helps what?' said the King.

'Mostly it helps in times of war,' said the tutor.

'Why's that?' said the King.

'Because, sir,' said the tutor, 'it will prove that we're not fighting a country. We're just fighting a random sent of persons, just like any country has to do when it's dealing with criminals.'

'And we can do that, simply by saying that these people are not "a people"?' said the King.

'All I can say again,' said the tutor, 'is that it helps.'

'But do you believe it?' said the King.

'What's that got to do with it?' said the tutor, 'the important thing is that we say it, not whether we believe it.'

'Oh yes, of course,' said the King.

'Excellent,' said the tutor.

ESCALATION

'The Emperor says, "We face the very real danger of a further regional escalation of conflict",' said the King to this tutor, 'he's obviously very worried.'

'I don't think so,' said the tutor.

'What do you mean, you "don't think so"?,' said the King, 'here it is, in black and white, 'we face a very real danger.'

'Yes, yes, yes,' said the tutor, 'of course he says that stuff but he doesn't believe a word of it.'

'Oh that's very cynical,' said the King, 'I didn't think you could be as cold-hearted and suspicious as that.'

'Well,' said the tutor, 'can you give me a single example of when the Emperor has actually done anything to prevent a 'regional escalation of conflict'?'

'I'm sure there are many examples,' said the King, 'I mean I've heard him or his envoys saying over and over again, that they are trying to keep things as peaceful as possible.'

'Yes,' said the tutor, 'but once again, you're not understanding what's going on here, sir. What the Emperor says and what the Emperor does, are two completely different things.'

'Oh really?' said the King, 'then explain to me what is it that he's doing that is different from what he's saying?'

'How about him giving us the excellent new spears and shields so that we can . . . how shall I put it? . . . escalate the conflict'?' said the tutor.

'I suppose that is one way of looking at it,' said the King.

'It's the only way,' said the tutor.

'I have to grant you, you do have a certain clarity when you approach these issues,' said the King, 'so you are in effect saying that we and the world should really take no notice of what the Emperor is saying?'

'Precisely,' said the tutor.

'Then why's he saying it?' said the King.

'So that people like you will believe what he says,' said the tutor, 'and then you'll think that he's the good guy in all this.'

'I hadn't thought of it that way,' said the King, 'thanks very much. You really are very good at this stuff, aren't you?'

'Thank you, sir,' said the tutor.

SOME PEOPLE ARE HURTING

'Some people are hurting, tutor,' said the King.

'You mean poor people?' said the King's tutor.

'No,' said the King, 'they are people who think that we are good and who do good things but who discover that we are not always good and sometimes do bad things.'

'Oh dear,' said the tutor, 'and you want me to worry about them?'

'I just think that we should bear them in mind,' said the King.

'Why?' said the tutor.

'Because they have our best interests at heart,' said the King.

'I don't think so,' said the tutor, 'I used to think so, but not anymore.'

'Don't we need them?' said the King.

'No,' said the tutor.

'Oh,' said the King, 'who do we need then?'

'We need people who are 100% with us,' said the tutor.

'What? No matter what we do?' said the King.

'Exactly, said the tutor.

CONDEMNATION

'What do you think about people condemning us?' said the King to his tutor.

'Two things,' said the tutor, 'one: we condemn everyone who condemns us. Two: condemning us doesn't matter anyway.'

'Really?' said the King, 'that doesn't make sense. If we're condemning them for condemning us, then obviously it matters.'

'I'm afraid you misunderstand what's going on,' said the tutor. 'There's always a rabble or mob who condemn us. These can be ignored. Then there are other kingdoms who condemn us. These can't be ignored but all that matters about them is what they'll tolerate.'

'Tolerate?' said the King, 'the point is, they're not tolerating. They're condemning.'

'Ah, and there you have it wrong, sir,' said the tutor, 'the whole point is that they're condemning AND tolerating. AND some of them, helping us too. We know that. They know that. And that's why we can carry on.'

'We can carry on?' said the King, 'Really?'

'Of course,' said the tutor.

'Oh that's good,' said the King.

A TRUCE

'When is a truce not a truce?' said the King to his tutor.

'Good question,' said the King's tutor, ' a truce is not a truce when we decide it's not a truce.'

'That sounds fair,' said the King, 'though I am interested in the idea that a truce is between two 'parties' as our lawyers put it.'

'What's that got to do with it?' said the tutor.

'Only that I thought two parties have to agree on what it is or isn't,' said the King.

'That's where you're wrong,' said the tutor, 'we define the terms of the truce. If the other side say that they disagree with our terms it's not a truce. If the other side agree with our terms, but we no longer agree with our terms, it's also not a truce.'

'Oh that's very good,' said the King, 'I really hadn't thought of that.'

'Thank you, sir,' said the tutor.

LOOKING GOOD

'We've got to put in a lot of work to ensure that we look good,' said the King's tutor.

'Really?' said the King, 'can't we just get on and do what we've got to do?'

'No,' said the tutor, 'because some people don't like what we've got to do.'

'Yes, but they're dunderheads and evil-minded ne'er-do-wells who hate us anyway,' said the King.

'But we still have to strive to ensure that we look good,' said the tutor. 'because there are waverers.'

'Oh yes,' said the King, 'and we don't like waverers, do we?'

'No,' said the tutor, 'we like non-apologetic supporters.'

'So how do you propose to stop the waverers wavering?' said the King.

'First of all, we remind the waverers that everyone we oppose is bad,' said the tutor.

'Of course,' said the King. 'What next?'

'Then we remind the waverers that we're good,' said the tutor.

'I was forgetting that for a moment,' said the King, 'is that it?'

'Yes,' said the tutor, 'but the point is that we have to keep on saying it.'

'I understand,' said the King.

'Good,' said the tutor.

THE ONLY WAY

'What's new today?' said the King to this tutor.
　'Not a lot,' said the King's tutor.
　'That's a shame,' said the King, 'no wars? No battles?'
　'Oh yes,' said the tutor, 'lots of that.'
　'How are we doing?' said the King.
　'Superbly,' said the tutor.
　'That's good,' said the King, 'any idea when they'll stop?'
　'No,' said the tutor.
　'Is there anything we could be doing other than wars and battles?' said the King.
　'No,' said the tutor, 'wars and battles are the only way.'
　'Do they work?' said the King.
　'How do you mean?' said the tutor.
　'Do they achieve what they set out achieve?' said the King.
　'Not usually,' said the tutor.
　'Does that matter?' said the King.
　'Not at all,' said the tutor.
　'So no news, then?' said the King.
　'Exactly,' said the tutor.

BING-BANGS

'The Emperor says that he's not going to give us that great big bing-bang,' said the King.

'Yes,' said the King's tutor.

'You don't seem worried,' said the King.

'Why should I be?' said the tutor.

'We need great big bing-bangs so we can eliminate the bad people,' said the King.

'But the Emperor has given us thousands of great big bing-bangs in the past and will give us thousands of great big bing-bangs in the future,' said the tutor.

'But we need great big bing-bangs NOW,' said the King.

'Relax, sir,' said the tutor, 'the Emperor is giving us lots of little bing-bangs.'

'I don't like it,' said the King, 'it feels like the Emperor doesn't love us anymore.'

'So what?' said the tutor, 'it was never about love.'

'Wasn't it?' said the King.

'Of course not,' said the tutor, 'it's about knowing that us being here, means that all the kings around about argue amongst themselves about what to do about us. That's good for the Emperor.'

'I wish I understood this stuff,' said the King.

'No need to,' said the tutor, 'it's just how it is.'

WHAT IT LOOKS LIKE

'You seem worried,' said the King to his tutor.

'Yes,' said the tutor.

'Can I help? What's troubling you?' said the King.

'Oh, nothing you can help me with,' said the tutor.

'Is it the news about the enemy?' said the King.

'Not directly,' said the tutor.

'Ah, let me guess,' said the King, 'you're worried that we've gone too far this time. We've overdone the scorched earth thing?'

'Not exactly,' said the tutor.

'I give up,' said the King, 'I can't think what it is.'

'I'm very worried that what we're doing is a very bad look,' said the tutor.

'What? The death and destruction, you mean?' said the King.

'Yes,' said the tutor.

'So you're not worried about what we're doing,' said the King, 'you're worried about what it looks like?'

'Exactly,' said the tutor.

'Well you're the clever one round here,' said the King, 'I'm sure if you concentrate you'll find a way of making it all look better.'

'Good point, sir,' said the tutor, 'so long as we can carry on doing what we're actually doing.'

'The scorched earth stuff, you mean?' said the King.

'Yes,' said the tutor.

'Oh yes we have to do that,' said the King.

'That's what I thought,' said the tutor. 'And if I may say so, sir, you're being very astute today.'

'Thank you, tutor,' said the King.

ACTIONS

'Now here's an interesting point, tutor,' said the King, 'in years to come, people will wonder whether it was a matter of "the world couldn't do anything about it", or "the world wouldn't do anything about it".'

'Yes, that is a very interesting point,' said the King's tutor.

'And do you think this in itself is an interesting intellectual point?' said the King, 'Or is it something that really matters right now?'

'Well,' said the tutor, 'certainly if we can have people walking about wondering about such things, it means there are fewer people trying to stop us.'

'I'm guessing there, tutor,' said the King, 'you're trying to say something about actions matter more than words.'

'Well, if the actions are happening right now, then it really doesn't matter what words are being argued over again and again and again, does it?' said the tutor.

'Well why do people do it, then?' said the King, 'I mean we're doing it right now.'

'Exactly,' said the tutor, 'and all the time we're getting on with the actions.'

'Jolly good,' said the King.

PRYING PEOPLE

'What would you say is your greatest achievement, tutor?' said the King.

'Keeping prying people out,' said the tutor.

'Interesting,' said the King, 'why do you think that has been so important?'

'By keeping prying people out, we stop the world knowing what's going on,' said the tutor.

'But the world knows what's going on,' said the King.

'You miss the point sir,' said the tutor.

'How so?' said the King.

'By keeping prying people out, we ensure that there is a furious debate about what is really going on,' said the tutor.

'Yes, I've seen that,' said the King.

'The point is, sir, that furious debate, all that hot air being generated helps us. People spend vast amounts of energy debating whether this or that did or did not happen, while leaving us free to carry on doing what we're doing.'

'But that energy is establishing the truth,' said the King.

'You're nearly there, but not quite,' said the tutor, 'because we keep the prying people out, there is an endless war of words about what we're really doing. In fact, there are people out there who accuse each other of being dangerous precisely because they say that others are getting it wrong. And then that lot accuse the others back saying the same thing. It's marvellous. One great feast of hot air, while we just carry on and no one really knows what's going on.'

'I think I follow you,' said the King.

'Our point – and I'll want you to keep saying this – is that we're good. So when prying people say that we've done bad things, we will simply say, 'but we're good' and that will overrule any hot air saying that we've done bad things.'

'As you say, "marvellous", tutor!' said the King.

KIND PEOPLE

'We're kind people aren't we, tutor?' said the King.

'Yes,' said the tutor, 'why do you ask?'

'I've heard rumours that there are some who say that we're not kind,' said the King.

'And what has caused them to make such foul accusations?' said the tutor.

'That we are moving tens of thousands of people from their homes,' said the King.

'Oh that,' said the tutor, 'then you must explain that we are doing that so that we can move those poor people out of harm's way. As you say, we are kind people.'

'However,' said the King, 'there are some who even question why it is we think we have the right to rule over a people and do such things.'

'Those who direct such comments at us, do not appreciate that we are engaged in a battle for civilisation itself,' said the tutor.

'Oh, are we?' said the King, 'I thought we were moving people out of harm's way.'

'We'll have a lesson on the battle for civilisation itself tomorrow, then,' said the tutor.

'I look forward to it,' said the King.

STARVING PEOPLE

'I'm hearing reports that the people are starving,' said the King.

'Whose reports?' said the King's tutor.

'Reports from various people,' said the King.

'That's where you're making a mistake,' said the tutor. 'You're going on about people starving when you should be going on about the kind of people who say that the people are starving.'

'Really?' said the King.

'Of course,' said the tutor. 'Ask yourself, what kind of people would say such terrible things about you. What kind of people would say that people in your country are starving?'

'Yes, I see,' said the King, 'they would be terrible people.'

'Indeed,' said the tutor, 'and I hope you put out an announcement telling people that.'

'Like, 'I'm horrified to learn that people are saying that people are starving'?' said the King.

'Good, but not good enough,' said the tutor. 'It would be better if you made no mention of the 'starving' bit.'

'Right,' said the King, 'how about this: 'I'm horrified to learn that people are saying terrible things about us.'

'Excellent,' said the tutor, 'you've got it.'

'Good,' said the King.

NUMBERS

'Do you like talking about numbers, tutor?' said the King.'

'Very much so,' said the tutor.

'I thought you did,' said the King, 'because you're very good at maths.'

'Actually, I'm not,' said the tutor.

'Oh?' said the King, 'then why do you like talking about numbers?'

'What I like about numbers,' said the tutor, 'is people arguing about them.'

'They do, don't they?' said the King, 'very annoying.'

'No,' said the tutor, 'quite the opposite. The more people argue about the numbers, the less anyone believes in them.'

'Not sure I follow you there,' said the King.

'The moment people start arguing about numbers people say to themselves, it's all rubbish. And that's good for us,' said the tutor.

'Is it?' said the King.

'Of course,' said the tutor, 'that means no one can blame us for what we do, because everyone says the numbers are rubbish.'

'Brilliant,' said the King.

'That's what I think,' said the tutor.

ARE WE BAD?

'What do we do when people say that we are bad?' said the King.

'We say that we're not as bad as that,' said the King's tutor.

'As bad as what?' said the King.

'As bad as they say we are,' said the tutor.

'Does that work?' said the King.

'Amazingly, it does,' said the tutor.

'How come?' said the King.

'People get so racked up about how bad we are, than when we say, "not as bad as that", people say, "Fair enough",' said the tutor.

'I had no idea it was simple as that,' said the King.

'Well, there is a bit more to it,' said the tutor, 'we have to do some spluttering.'

'What's that?' said the King.

'We have to splutter that we are outraged with the people who've said we're bad,' said the tutor.

'How does that work?' said the King.

'It makes us sound virtuous,' said the tutor.

'Even though we might be bad?' said the King.

'Could you keep your voice down,' said the tutor, 'we never admit that we could be bad.'

'Understood' said the King.

AN ANNOUNCEMENT

'You must make an announcement that you are very sad that other people haven't supported us in our time of need,' said the King's tutor.

'But they have,' said the King.

'I don't think you've figured this right,' said the tutor, 'the point is we feel very isolated,'

'But we're not,' said the King.

'What you're saying is very unhelpful,' said the tutor.

'But everyone can see that there are some very important people helping us,' said the King, 'I can't just go out and there and say, "No one is helping us",'

'What you say is that we feel betrayed and alone,' said the tutor.

'Do we?' said the King.

'That's beside the point,' said the tutor.

'Is it?' said the King.

'Now go out there and make that announcement,' said the tutor.

'OK,' said the King.

THE RIGHT THING

'Tutor,' said the King to his tutor, 'I know you think that what we're doing is absolutely the right thing, but do you think we could have done anything else instead?'

'Absolutely not,' said the tutor, 'what we're doing is the only thing we could be doing. There is no alternative.'

'I understand,' said the King, 'but can I ask whether we have evidence that what we're doing works?'

'Why are you asking that?' said the tutor. 'Asking questions like that undermines what we're doing.'

'But shouldn't we have some general kind of idea that what we're doing works?' said the King, 'Otherwise, we might be making a mistake.'

'Not only is there no alternative,' said the tutor, 'but we're doing this in the best possible way. I've looked at examples from other situations like ours and we're behaving in the world's best ever way. No one has been as good at doing this as we are.'

'That's very powerful,' said the King. 'It makes me proud to think that we're doing things so well. So why do people say that what we're doing is wrong?'

'I've explained that to you before,' said the tutor, 'it's because they hate us.'

'Oh yes, I remember,' said the King, 'so it's full steam ahead. On we go, eh? '

'That's it,' said the tutor.

FRAMING

'Do you understand 'framing' and 'reframing', sir?' said the King's tutor.

'Picture frames, you mean?' said the King.

'No,' said the tutor, 'this is about framing and re-framing what's going on.'

'Really?' said the King, 'how do you do that?'

'Indeed,' said the tutor, 'that's the nub of the matter.'

'Go on,' said the King.

'Well let's say that Jack has a fight with Jim,' said the tutor, 'how I tell that story will alter the way people view that fight.'

'How?' said the King.

'If I tell you that Jack is a bully and picks fights on a regular basis,' said the tutor, 'you will immediately have a view of this fight. If, on the other hand, I say that Jim is a bully and picks fights on a regular basis, you will immediately have a different view.'

'That's very interesting,' said the King, 'I had never thought of that before. By the way, what happened to Jack and Jim?'

'Jack killed Jim,' said the tutor.

'Oh dear,' said the King, 'so why are we talking about framing and re-framing?'

'Because if Jim is on our side, then we must make clear that Jack is to blame,' said the tutor, 'but if Jack is on our side, then we must make clear that Jack is not to blame.'

'I'm confused,' said the King, 'but it sounds as if you've got it very well sorted.'

'I have,' said the tutor.

WORDS AND DEEDS

'We really do need to have that conversation again about words and deeds,' said the King to his tutor.

'How so?' said the tutor, 'tell me what's concerning you.'

'I was brought up to believe that words can be bad and horrible but they aren't as harmful as deeds,' said the King.

'Can you give me examples?' said the tutor.

'Well let me ask you about an extreme example,' said the King, 'Jack kills Jim. That's a deed. Meanwhile, John says Jack is a bastard. That would be words, wouldn't it?'

'I see what you're driving at,' said the tutor, 'but I really need to know more about Jack and John before I commit myself.'

'Oh,' said the King, 'I thought it would be quite straightforward.'

'No,' said the tutor, 'you see, what if Jack is you?'

'Go on,' said the King.

'Well,' said the tutor, 'you're the King. Saying horrible things about you is dangerous. it could undermine the monarchy and threaten the whole nation.'

'Yes,' said the King.

'What's more, I want to know how John is being horrible about you. Is he talking about your background?' said the tutor.

'Well let's say he is,' said the King.

'Exactly, 'said the tutor, 'and we can't let people be derogatory about your background, can we sir?'

'No,' said the King, 'that would be hate and we would want to punish that,'

'Exactly,' said the tutor, 'so you see when we weigh it up, it may turn out that though you killing Jim is unfortunate, we might in the long run see that the way John was talking about you is heinous.'

'Thanks for clearing that up, tutor,' said the King.

MISSING THE POINT

'I have a document here,' said the King to his tutor, 'that says we are fighting a humane war.'

'Excellent,' said the tutor, 'I wish more people would see that.'

'Yes,' said the King, 'though it did get me wondering if we really are being humane.'

'I think you need to realign your concerns,' said the tutor.

'How so?' said the King.

'We could spend years investigating whether this really is or is not a humane war,' said the tutor. 'Spending hours and hours trying to figure out whether it's true or not is a waste of time.'

'You surprise me,' said the King, 'I thought it was our duty to investigate a statement like that and try to determine whether it's true or not.'

'Oh dear,' said the tutor, 'there you go again: missing the point.'

'Enlighten me then,' said the King.

'Put it like this,' said the tutor, 'no war is humane. It's an absurd proposition.'

'Then why say it?' said the King.

'So that enough people who believe we are good, will have a word to say when we are being accused of being bad people,' said the tutor.

'But then the people who say it's not a humane war come up with arguments to support their view,' said the King.

'Exactly,' said the tutor, 'they get dragged into arguing about something that was absurd in the first place.'

'I think I see,' said the King.

A VERY HUMANE WAR

'What do you think of the war so far, tutor?' said the King to his tutor.

'I think it's a very humane war,' said the tutor.

'You surprise me,' said the King, 'I was thinking that there are a lot of people being killed.'

'Yes,' said the tutor, 'that's humane.'

POWER

'I am very powerful, aren't I, tutor?' said the King to his tutor.

'Well, let's think about that, shall we?' said the tutor, 'do you understand the idea that your power might depend on other factors?'

'Like the weather, you mean?' said the King.

'I was thinking more along the lines of the kinds of power exerted by those with greater power than you,' said the tutor.

'Oh you mean the Emperor?' said the King.

'Yes,' said the tutor.

'Oh he's just a bumbling busybody,' said the King, 'your clever plans tie him in knots.'

'I don't think you have that right,' said the tutor, 'better by far, to ask yourself the question, 'Why is the Emperor so involved in our affairs?'

'Because he's a busybody,' said the King, 'I explained that.'

'I'm afraid, sir, that doesn't explain it,' said the tutor. 'You see, the Emperor has what we call 'strategic interests',' said the tutor.

'What's that got to do with us?' said the King.

'Perhaps think of it like this: we're here because he's here,' said the tutor.

'And if he wasn't here?' said the King.

'Think about that for a moment, sir,' said the tutor.

'Oh dear,' said the King.

BUSYBODIES

'Tutor,' said the King, 'can you think of a situation in which everyone is the enemy?'

'It's possible,' said the tutor, 'what do you have in mind?'

'What if, for example,' said the King, 'we need to liquidate the enemy over there?'

'Go on,' said the tutor.

'Well, won't we find that part of the problem we would face with a job like that is that all sorts of busybodies would want to monitor what we're doing? said the King.

'Yes, that's a good point,' said the tutor.

'And these busybodies spread bad news about us . . .' said the King.

'Yes indeed, they do,' said the tutor.

'Well what do we do about that?' said the King.

'If I get you right,' said the tutor, 'you're suggesting that we have to regard these busybodies in just the same way as we regard the enemy itself.'

'What concerns me though,' said the King, 'is that people will say that busybodies have rights of some kind or another and if we're seen to be eliminating these busybodies, it will reflect badly on us.'

'Oh I don't think you would need to worry about that,' said the tutor, 'our systems of sharing information are much more widely distributed than anything that the busybodies (or their supporters) can muster.'

'Oh that's alright then,' said the King.

'Yes,' said the tutor.

PEACE

'At some point, we have to make peace with our enemies, don't we?' said the King to his tutor.

'I'm not so sure,' said the King's tutor.

'You mean we can go on and on and on forever?' said the King.

'Yes,' said the tutor.

'How come?' said the King.

'We have bigger and better swords,' said the tutor.

'So we keep winning?' said the King.

'Well, if not actually winning,' said the tutor, 'it's not actually losing.'

'But what if there are all those documents to do with having a treaty?' said the King, 'shouldn't we stop then?'

'There are ways round them,' said the tutor.

'Go on,' said the King.

'It works like this,' said the tutor, 'we come up with a peace plan. The other side agree to it. Just as we're about to sign, we come up with extra bits that they didn't agree to.'

'What's the point of that?' said the King.

'Do try to concentrate, sir,' said the tutor, 'that way we keep on and on and on not actually winning but not actually losing either.'

'Is there no other way of doing things?' said the King.

'No,' said the tutor.

'Fair enough,' said the King.

VAGUENESS

'Do we know how many of the other side have died?' said the King to his tutor.

'What a strange question,' said the King's tutor.

'I was just curious,' said the King.

'Well, for starters, we say that we don't know,' said the tutor.

'Can you give me a rough idea?' said the King.

'Even if I told you what that rough idea is,' said the tutor, 'it would be a great mistake to tell the people.'

'Why's that?' said the King.

'I don't think you understand the virtues of vagueness,' said the tutor.

'I don't think I've ever heard of that,' said the King.

'The virtues of vagueness,' said the tutor, 'are that everyone argues over what we're being vague about. Some come up with one figure, others come up with another. So no one knows for certain.'

'What do we say, though?' said the King.

'Nothing,' said the tutor, 'please try to follow this. We benefit from there being no agreed number. In the place of a number, there is argument, dispute, doubt, speculation and . . . as I said, vagueness.'

'But one day, people will find out the number, won't they?' said the King.

'I very much doubt it,' said the tutor.

'And that's good for us?' said the King.

'You've got it,' said the tutor.

THAT CORNER

'I've heard that some judges somewhere or another have said that we shouldn't be in the corner over there,' said the King to his tutor.

'Oh judges!' said the King's tutor, 'they'll say anything that they're paid to say.'

'It does bother me somewhat though,' said the King.

'It shouldn't,' said the tutor, 'remember that that corner over there is ours.'

'Is it?' said the King, 'I thought we were in that corner over there in order to keep us safe over here.'

'Yes,' said the tutor, 'it's what we said, but in fact, that corner over there has belonged to us for thousands of years.'

'Apart from the times when we weren't there, perhaps?' said the King.

'Good point,' said the tutor, 'we were indeed ejected from that corner over there some time or another a long, long time ago. That's why we're back in the corner over there.'

'Hmm, that sounds very good,' said the King, 'but I went there once and there were some people there who aren't our people.'

'Exactly,' said the tutor, 'and our job is to make sure that they aren't there.'

'How will we do that?' said the King.

'We have very good horses and carts,' said the tutor.

'And we put these people on the carts?' said the King.

'Exactly,' said the tutor.

'That's very good,' said the King, 'I thought you'd think of something. You always do.'

'Thank you, sir,' said the tutor.

LAST CHANCE SALOON

'Tutor,' said the King, 'are we in the last chance saloon?'

'In a way, yes' said the King's tutor.

'And what do you think about being in here?' said the King.

'We're in an interesting point in our overall project,' said the tutor.

'But it's not going very well, is it?' said the King.

'Well, that all depends on what you mean by "well",' said the tutor.

'I mean "well" so that we lived in peace and security,' said the King.

'Oh that!' said the tutor, 'Being over-ambitious was always your problem. Don't aim so high.'

'Where should I aim?' said the King.

'How about . . . "being King"?' said the tutor.

'Is that it?' said the King.

'Well it's better than not being King, isn't it?' said the tutor.

'Yes, I suppose so,' said the King.

'There you are, then,' said the tutor.

'So we should just carry on?' said the King.

'Of course,' said the tutor.

'Even if it is the last chance saloon?' said the King.

'Yes, indeed,' said the tutor, 'even in the last chance saloon. We can sit in here for a long, long time, sir.'

'Oh good,' said the King.

PICTURES

'How do you feel about pictures, tutor?' said the King to his tutor.

'I think pictures of you or me are fine, sir,' said the King's tutor.

'No, tutor,' said the King, 'I was thinking of pictures of the battlefield.'

'Ah yes,' said the tutor, 'that's a very different matter. Whose pictures are these?'

'Well,' said the King, 'I understand that one or two of the pictures are ours, but there are pictures being painted by people friendly to the enemy.'

'So I understand,' said the tutor. 'Well, what we say,' the tutor added, 'is that all pictures painted by the enemy should be doubted.'

'Doubted?' said the King.

'Yes,' said the tutor, 'we have to make it clear that everything and anything that the enemy do by way of producing pictures might not be true.'

'But what if they are true?' said the King.

'This may be the case,' said the tutor, 'but we have to ensure that people wonder if they're true. At which point, they will wonder if everything else the enemy says is true. And that will be good for us.'

'So we say, 'The pictures are not true,'?' said the King.

'We do,' said the tutor.

'That's very clear,' said the King.

CONCERN

'Tutor,' said the King, 'our allies have expressed concern.'

'That's good,' said the King's tutor.

'Good?' said the King, 'I don't get that. It worries me that they've expressed concern.'

'Don't be worried, sir,' said the tutor, 'when they express concern, that means that they don't actually do anything.'

'Really?' said the King, 'I thought that expressing concern was a lead up to them doing something.'

'That's where you've got it wrong,' said the tutor, 'they express concern INSTEAD of doing something.'

'Why would they do that?' said the King.

'So that after the thing they expressed concern about is over, they can say that they expressed concern,' said the tutor.

'What a good idea,' said the King.

'That's what I think,' said the tutor.

THE NEWS

'The news is not too good, is it, tutor?' said the King.

'No sir,' said the King's tutor.

'What should we do, do you think?' said the King.

'Make some news ourselves,' said the tutor.

'Really?' said the King, 'how can we do that?'

'Well, if I went out and shot someone who I said was a spy,' said the tutor, 'that would be making news.'

'Yes, yes,' said the King, 'but that would be illegal and you would get arrested.'

'Possibly but not certainly,' said the tutor. 'Even so, I take your point, it's not worth the risk.'

'So what then?' said the King.

'Well, how about if there was an event organised by the people we don't like' said the tutor, 'and I went along and started shouting?'

'That sounds very boring,' said the King.

'Wait a moment, sir,' said the tutor. 'What if, when I started shouting, that made people angry? And they started shouting back, and even threatening me?'

'That wouldn't be very nice at all,' said the King, 'I think you've got this very wrong. Bad idea, tutor.'

'I don't think so,' said the tutor, 'because, all I would have done is do a bit of shouting and now, all of a sudden, there are hundreds of people picking on me. They start to look like a mob, a baying mob.'

'But no one would know about this baying mob,' said the King, 'it would be a silly idea.'

'Ah, that's where you're wrong,' said the tutor, 'it could be arranged that some of our scribes would be there to see it all, and they would tell the story of how a poor little chap had been set upon by a baying mob. And this would prove just how bad these people are.'

'You've forgotten something though,' said the King, 'the scribes would know that it was you, and when they wrote the story, they would say, 'The King's tutor started all this.'

'If I may say so, sir,' said the tutor, 'what you're saying there is not as clever as you think. Remember, these are our scribes! We make sure that they don't mention that it was the King's tutor who started it. It was just a poor chap who raised his voice a little at some event or other, and then he got picked on.'

'I'm beginning to see where you're going with this,' said the King, 'so in the end, this would be quite good news, because it would make others. who we don't like, look bad.'

'Exactly,' said the tutor.

'Oh no,' said the King, 'I've thought of another snag. What if there were people there who recognised you, and started telling the scribes that it was you?'

'Hmm,' said the tutor, 'that's actually a very good point. However, we can trust it such that even if it became known that it was me, a blanket of silence would fall on everything, such that our good people would not know or understand what had really happened. Either that, or they would be just mildly confused and indifferent to it all anyway.'

'You do very good work, tutor, I must say,' said the King.

'Thank you for saying so, sir,' said the tutor.

SAVING LIVES

'Today,' said the King's tutor, 'we're going to talk about saving lives.'

'That's nice,' said the King, 'at last we can talk about the good things we do.'

'The first thing to remember about saving lives,' said the tutor, 'is that we do this through war.'

'Yes,' said the King, 'you mean we have our apothecaries and physicians who administer medicaments and salves to our soldiers' wounds.'

'Not exactly,' said the tutor, 'I was thinking more about what happens in times of battle.'

'Go on,' said the King.

'Well we have swords, cannons, pikes, lances and arrows,' said the tutor.

'We do,' said the King.

'When we attack we use these,' said the tutor.

'We do,' said the King, 'I don't follow where you're going with this.'

'When we attack a city, say, we use these,' said the tutor.

'Of course we do,' said the King, 'that's where the enemy is.'

'What I want you to think about here, though,' said the tutor, 'is just think: if we wanted to we could kill everyone in the city. But we don't.'

'That's true,' said the King.

'Today's lesson is about saving lives' said the tutor. 'I've just demonstrated how war saves lives.'

'On account of us not killing everybody,' said the King.

'Exactly,' said the tutor.

'It's been a good lesson today,' said the King, 'I'm most grateful to you.'

A GREATER POWER

'Tell me tutor, do you ever have a sense that there's a bigger power than us?' said the King to his tutor.

'God, you mean?' said the tutor.

'No, not God,' said the King.

'Who then?' said the tutor.

'You know, a great power,' said the King.

'Well of course we have allies,' said the tutor.

'I know that,' said the King, 'but I was thinking that maybe one or two of these allies might be a kind of bigger power than us.'

'I don't think it's wise to go down this route, sir,' said the tutor.

'It's just that every now and then,' said the King, 'I get the impression that maybe we're not in charge of our own destiny.'

'Well, put it this way,' said the tutor, 'if that were true, the best thing to do would be to keep quiet about it.'

'Why's that?' said the King.

'Because we want the world to know that we're standing on our own two feet,' said the tutor, 'protecting our people, doing what we're destined to do, in this great land of ours.'

'Yes, I get that,' said the King, 'but what if all that is just so that this greater power than us, gets its own way?'

'It's possible,' said the King, 'and if it were true, it doesn't really matter because we're the beneficiaries, aren't we?'

'Yes,' said the King, 'but then it's us that gets whacked, if trouble breaks out.'

'That doesn't matter in the long-term,' said the tutor, 'because we can always take advantage of that and get what we want, and even more of what we want.'

'Because it suits this greater power?' said the King.

'Exactly,' said the tutor.

'So we're all doing well out of it,' said the King.

'Yes indeed,' said the tutor, 'though not exactly all. But all of us on this side of the argument, yes.'

'Yes,' said the King.

POSITION

'What kind of position are we in, tutor?' said the King to his tutor.

'Pretty good,' said the King's tutor.

'Hmm, I'm a bit concerned,' said the King.

'How come?' said the tutor.

'We don't seem to be winning,' said the King.

'That doesn't matter,' said the tutor.

'Don't be ridiculous,' said the King, 'of course it matters.'

'No,' said the tutor, 'all that matters is that it's going on and on.'

'I don't follow you,' said the King.

'If it goes on and on,' said the tutor, 'it means that we don't have to have a treaty.'

'What?' said the King, 'we have to have a treaty. Everyone has treaties.'

'Not us,' said the tutor, 'we can just go on and on and not have a treaty.'

'But there has to be an end,' said the King.

'Not so,' said the tutor, 'if we go on and on, in the end we keep what we get.'

'I think that's very unlikely,' said the King.

'Really?' said the tutor, 'I think if you look at what's happened in the past that's exactly what's happened: we keep what we get.'

'Hmm, said the King, 'I hadn't seen it that way before.'

'There you are sir,' said the tutor, 'on we go. On and on and on and on.'

'Seems the best way,' said the King.

EXCELLENT WEAPONS

'We have excellent weapons, don't we tutor?' said the King.

'Indeed we do,' said the King's tutor.

'Remind me of what we've got,' said the King, 'I have to admit, it makes me feel very proud of our nation and our history, when you tell me about such things.'

'Well, sir,' said the tutor, 'I would like to tell you about our greatest weapon of all.'

'What's that?' said the King.

'It's an extraordinary spear,' said the tutor, 'once launched, it only kills enemy soldiers.'

'But what if there are people who are not soldiers who are in its way?' said the King.

'Good point,' said the tutor. 'And indeed, it's the whole point. As this spear flies towards a soldier, and if there's a non-soldier in the way, this spear will fly round the non-soldier and head on towards the enemy soldier. It will miss the non-soldier altogether.'

'That's amazing,' said the King.

'Not only amazing,' said the tutor, 'it shows what sort of people we are.'

'How so?' said the King.

'It shows that we are good, kind and humane people,' said the tutor.

'Oh good,' said the King.

A SECRET WEAPON

'I've thought of a secret weapon, sir,' said the King's tutor to the King.

'Oh yes?' said the King, 'that sounds good. What is it?'

'We put poison in the bread,' said the tutor, 'and the enemy soldiers will eat it.'

'Sounds good,' said the King, 'though I've got a little bit of concern.'

'Really?' said the tutor, 'what's that?'

'How do we know that the bread will only get eaten by soldiers?' said the King.

'I don't think that matters,' said the tutor.

'Doesn't it?' said the King.

'Well, put it this way,' said the tutor, 'it will be eaten by soldiers because the bread goes to where the soldiers live.'

'Yes, I know that,' said the King, 'but there are other people living where the soldiers live.'

'Yes,' said the tutor, 'these things do happen.'

'Well what do we do then?' said the King.

'First of all we say these other people didn't die,' said the tutor, 'then we say, that if these other people died, we're sorry, but we're fighting for our survival here, and then we say, that it's the enemy soldiers' fault.'

'That seems to deal with most of the criticism we're likely to get,' said the King.

'Yes,' said the tutor, 'it's important that we know how to handle these things.'

ATTACK IS DEFENCE

'Do you think we come across as being very warlike, tutor?' said the King.

'There's no reason why we should,' said the King's tutor, 'why do you ask?'

'Oh just a thought I had,' said the King, 'because we are doing quite a lot of fighting.'

'Indeed we are,' said the tutor, 'but every bit of it is on account of having to defend ourselves.'

'Of course,' said the King, 'I know that's what we say we're doing but is it all really defending ourselves? Isn't some of it attack?'

'Yes indeed,' said the tutor, 'but attack is defence.'

'Is it?' said the King, 'I thought attack was attack.'

'An easy mistake to make,' said the tutor, 'but you have to remember that we have to abide by guidelines and convince people of the necessity of our actions.'

'And do people believe us?' said the King.

'It doesn't really matter whether they do or they don't,' said the tutor.

'Really not?' said the King.

'No,' said the tutor, 'it doesn't matter so long as they let us do what we're doing.'

'I think I get this,' said the King, 'and then the people we've said this stuff to about defending ourselves, they just go about saying we're defending ourselves? Is that it?'

'Indeed it is,' said the tutor.

'Very good,' said the King, 'so we've got right on our side, then.'

'We have,' said the tutor.

ON THE BRINK

'I need you to explain to the world that we are on the brink,' said the King's tutor to the King.

'Very well,' said the King, 'but I think I need a bit more information than that.'

'Like what?' said the tutor.

'Like what we are on the brink of,' said the King.

'We are on the brink of the end,' said the tutor.

'Are we though?' said the King.

'You need to concentrate on what you say, not on what you mean,' said the tutor.

'But what I say has to make some kind of sense,' said the King.

'Not necessarily,' said the tutor, 'sometimes what you say can create a sensation rather than sense.'

'So if I say, "we're on the brink", people won't wonder what this brink is?' said the King.

'Probably not,' said the tutor. 'Instead they will just have a sense that everything is near an edge or an end. You are making a picture in people's minds. People will see themselves on the edge of a cliff or a crevasse.'

'You're making me feel uneasy now,' said the King.

'Good,' said the tutor, 'and remember, when you step out in front of the people, they look up to you, as a purveyor of truth.'

'If only they knew, eh?' said the King.

'Shhhh,' said the tutor.

'Agreed,' said the King.

NAMES

'What do you think about names?' said the King to his tutor.

'They're very important,' said the tutor.

'Yes,' said the King, 'that's what I thought. Are our people's names important?'

'Yes,' said the tutor, 'very important.'

'Good,' said the King.

'And we must remember these names if they have sacrificed themselves for the honour of our country.'

'Oh yes,' said the King, 'we must. All those who fall on the field of battle, must be remembered.'

'Oh let me stop there you, sir,' said the tutor.

'Mmm?' said the King, 'Is there a problem?'

'Yes indeed, there is,' said the tutor, 'you said "all those who fall".'

'I did,' said the King, 'there is a nobility in laying down one's life for one's country.'

'Yes,' said the tutor, 'but that's when it's in honour of our country, sir. Not everyone on the field of battle is laying down their life for our country.'

'Ah yes,' said the King, 'you're referring to those on the other side.'

'Indeed I am,' said the tutor.

'So what do we do about them?' said the King.

'Good question,' said the tutor, 'and my way of answering it, is by way of talking about names.'

'Go on,' said the King.

'What we do is make sure that when our men die, their names are announced in full,' said the tutor.

'So you said. And . . . er . . . the others?' said the King.

'We make sure that their names are not announced,' said the tutor.

'And we do that because?' said the King.

'So that people understand what matters,' said the tutor.

'Or rather: who matters,' said the King.

'Very good, sir,' said the tutor, 'you're doing very well in these lessons these days.'

'Thank you,' said the King.

REPORTS

'Have you seen these?' said the King to this tutor.

'You look worried, sir,' said the tutor, 'what are they?'

'They're reports, tutor,' said the King, 'reports of what people are saying about us.'

'Go on,' said the tutor, 'and do try not to look so worried about it.'

'These reports,' said the King, 'say that people are "not happy" with what we're doing.'

'And?' said the tutor.

'This one here,' said the King, 'says that they're "a bit unhappy". A bit unhappy! It's unbearable that people are saying things like that.'

'I think you need to take stock of the situation, sir,' said the tutor, 'it's just words.'

'But what words, eh!' said the King. ' "Not happy" and "a bit unhappy". I'm shuddering thinking about it.'

'Sir,' said the tutor, 'relax. There is no need for this kind of anxiety. I put it to you again, what are any of these critics actually going to do? Answer me that.'

'Nothing, I suppose,' said the King.

'And there you have it,' said the tutor. 'It's just "da-dee-da-dee-da-dee-da . . . a little bit unhappy". It makes about as much difference to what we do as a fly being cross that he forgot to have a piss.'

'I haven't looked at it like that,' said the King, 'you see, I was stung by the criticism.'

'Exactly,' said the tutor.

'But hang on,' said the King, 'why are they doing it? Why are they so critical of us?'

'The main reason,' said the tutor, 'is to keep their friends happy. Whatever they say about US, is really a code for what they want the people in their countries to think about THEM.'

'And the other reason?' said the King.

'People hate us not for what we do, but for who we are,' said the tutor.

'You mean that we could do anything and they would still hate us?' said the King.

'Yes,' said the tutor.

'We could invent a new way for the whole world to have clean water, and they would still hate us?' said the King.

'Yep,' said the tutor.

'Oh well,' said the King, 'now you've put it like that, we might as well just carry on doing what we're doing.'

'Exactly,' said the tutor, 'you've got it.'

'Thanks, tutor,' said the King.

GOOD PEOPLE

'We're good people, aren't we, tutor?' said the King to his tutor.

'Yes we are,' said the tutor, 'but why do you ask?'

'Because I was thinking that if we're good people, we can't do bad things, can we?' said the King.

'Broadly speaking, I would agree with you there,' said the tutor, 'but there are some other aspects we need to consider.'

'Really?' said the King.

'Yes,' said the tutor, 'you see, for many years that has been our position. "We are good people. We don't do bad things. We haven't done bad things. Bad people do bad things to us. End of".'

'Yes,' said the King, 'I've heard myself say, "We're good people. How come you're saying we do bad things? How illogical is that!" It's worked up till now.'

'Exactly,' said the tutor, 'but now we have to have another approach. What we say now, is "there are rare occasions when we do bad things".'

'Oh,' said the King, 'that ruins everything.'

'Not so,' said the tutor, 'you're not thinking this through, sir. What we say now, is, "we're good people. Sometimes we do bad things but listen everybody, if we are good people doing bad things, that must be because we're doing the bad things for the right reasons".'

'Wow,' said the King, 'that's quite complicated.'

'Not so,' said the tutor, 'you see, our job now is to show the world that we're ridding the world of the bad people. Why are we doing this? Because we're the good people. Get it, sir?'

'My oh my,' said the King, 'so we're being bad in order to be good. That's amazing.'

'It is indeed,' said the tutor.

VALUES

'Can we talk about "values", tutor?' said the King to his tutor.

'Good idea,' said the tutor, 'but why now?'

'I've heard people say that what's going on now is a fight over values,' said the King.

'Yes,' said the tutor, 'I'm cautious about that.'

'How so?' said the King.

'Well,' said the tutor, 'I prefer to say that we're people defending ourselves. More of a military question.'

'I see,' said the King, 'but values come into it, don't they?'

'I see where you're going with this,' said the tutor, 'but we have to be careful about going on and on about values.'

'Why?' said the King.

'Let me put it like this,' said the tutor, 'we can of course say that our values are better than theirs. And we'll find plenty of people, loyal scribes to agree with us. Some of our greatest philosophers will write screeds on it, and everyone will nod sagely and say, yes indeed, but even so, I have a nagging feeling that there are problems with this approach.'

'And these feelings are . . . ?' said the King.

'The moment the focus is on values,' said the tutor, 'people will look closely at our values as well as theirs.'

'Of course,' said the King, 'and that's where we win.'

'That's the theory,' said the tutor, 'but when it widens out into how all our allies and friends behave – as opposed to all their allies and friends – it stops being quite so clear cut.'

'You shock me, tutor,' said the King, 'we are blameless.'

'We say we are,' said the tutor, 'and it's good that we do. Whether we are or not, is another matter. Next time, let's talk about ends and means.'

'Yes, let's,' said the King.

A PROCLAMATION

'I have written a proclamation,' said the King's tutor.

'Oh good,' said the King, 'can you summarise it for me?'

'It would be preferable that you read the whole proclamation, sir,' said the tutor, 'but if you can't or won't, I'll give you the main points.'

'Go ahead,' said the King.

'In my proclamation,' said the tutor, 'I concede that we have killed many thousands of innocent people.'

'Oh Lord God, no,' said the King, 'that's a mistake. Can't we go back to the position where we said we hadn't killed thousands of innocent people?'

'Please bear with me,' said the tutor, 'I have a point to make.'

'Sorry, do go on,' said the King.

'The point is,' said the tutor, 'is that we are the standard bearers for goodness and virtue.'

'Are we?' said the King.

'Of course,' said the tutor, 'you're good. I'm good. We are virtuous.'

'Hmm,' said the King.

'And our enemies are terrible, evil people who kill innocent people in their thousands,' said the tutor.

'But you just said that we kill innocent people in their thousands too,' said the King.

'Yes, but we do that as good and virtuous people,' said the tutor, 'not as terrible evil people.

'Oh I see, that must be a crucial difference for the innocent people being killed,' said the King.

'Exactly,' said the tutor, 'think how much better it must be for an innocent person being killed to know that they're being killed by a good and virtuous person as opposed to being killed by a terrible, evil person.'

'I think that's very clear,' said the King, 'thank you, tutor.'

CIVILISATION

'Do you think we represent civilisation?' said the King.

'Most certainly,' said the tutor, 'we have the civilised values of thousands of years behind us.'

'Oh that's good,' said the King, 'and are we recognised as such?'

'That's an interesting point,' said the tutor, 'because ironically, for thousands of years, we were regarded as the devil incarnate, outcast god-killers.'

'And then we became the opposite?' said the King.

'Indeed we did,' said the tutor, 'in a matter of years we have become the banner-bearers for all that's good about civilisation, particularly in this part of the world.'

'That's a relief,' said the King.

'And of course, we have taken on the job of fighting for civilisation,' said the tutor.

'Yes,' said the King, 'I like that, and we do it in civilised ways, don't we tutor?'

'Again and again and again,' said the tutor, 'we are spreading civilisation all the time, thoroughly and vigorously.'

'Do people appreciate this?' said the King.

'Surprisingly, some don't,' said the tutor, 'they berate us for being so thorough and vigorous.'

'What do you say to that?' said the King.

'I remind them that they are reverting to the times when they regarded us as the devil incarnate,' said the tutor.

'You're very good at this, aren't you?' said the King.

'I like to think I am,' said the tutor.

A MESS

'The battlefield is in a bit of a mess, isn't it, tutor?' said the King to his tutor.

'Yes indeed,' said the tutor, 'but things are going well.'

'Are they?' said the King, 'but there's nothing but churned up mud, spears and shields. And all those huts where those people lived. What a mess it all is.'

'You're not thinking ahead, sir,' said the tutor.

'Ahead?' said the King.

'Are you not aware that the battleground overlooks the sea?' said the tutor.

'No, I hadn't noticed that,' said the King.

'There is a beautiful view of the shoreline and the sea, twinkling in the sun,' said the tutor, 'it would be a perfect place for you to have a palace.'

'O that does sound very nice,' said the King, 'but what about the mess?'

'Don't worry your head about that,' said the tutor, 'we can clear that up.'

'And the huts?' said the King.

'And the huts,' said the tutor.

THE CORRECT ANSWER

'Are we interested in peace?' said the King to his tutor.

'We say we are,' said the tutor.

'That's not an answer to my question,' said the King.

'It's the correct answer when it comes to what we say to the rest of the world,' said the tutor.

'Alright,' said the King, 'it's just that I have a teeny tiny feeling that we're not interested in peace.'

'What makes you say that?' said the tutor.

'Well, the other day, you said that we are fighting for civilisation,' said the King, 'it's our values versus theirs, and all that.'

'Yes,' said the tutor, 'that's absolutely true.'

'Well,' said the King, 'I've figured out that if we're in this epic struggle, asserting our civilised values, then it's not peace we're looking for. We're looking to . . . er . . . assert our civilised values.'

'And when we have asserted our civilised values,' said the tutor, 'there'll be peace.'

'So the whole thing depends on us winning,' said the King.

'Of course,' said the tutor.

'But what if, in winning, we do it in ways that are not civilised?' said the King.

'So be it,' said the tutor, 'ends justify means, remember, sir!'

'Yes,' said the King, 'I think so.'

'On we go,' said the tutor.

'On we go,' said the King.

OTHER MOTIVES

'What do you think of people who describe what's going on?' said the King.

'That depends on their motive for doing so,' said the King's tutor.

'Even if they're accurate in what they're describing?' said the King.

'Most certainly,' said the tutor, 'accuracy is one thing and we support accuracy.'

'Good,' said the King.

'But sometimes we can discern something obsessive, something over-eager in the accuracy,' said the tutor.

'You mean that these people doing the describing are overly focussed in what they're doing?' said the King.

'Exactly,' said the tutor, 'and it makes us realise that they're doing it for other motives.'

'Really?' said the King.

'Yes,' said the tutor.

'Interesting, said the King.

'Very,' said the tutor.

SUPREME POWER

'I have supreme power, don't I?' said the King to his tutor.

'Yes and no,' said the tutor.

'I don't like the way you said that,' said the King, 'what's this "no" thing?'

'Well, sir,' said the tutor, 'it's useful to talk of your supreme power. People believe it. People respect it. And if they don't respect it, we remind people of it. '

'I don't think you're answering my question,' said the King, 'what's the "no" bit?'

'Yes, sir,' said the tutor, 'but this is where we have to talk about the Emperor.'

'And?' said the King.

'It's very complicated, sir,' said the tutor, 'but I could show you the Chancellor's accounts, I could show you the Lord High Armourer's weaponry invoices, but you really wouldn't be interested.'

'I'm not following you,' said the King.

'The Emperor's signature is on all of it,' said the tutor.

You mean,' said the King, 'that I owe all my power and wealth to the Emperor?

'Now that you put it like that,' said the tutor, 'yes.'

'Well obviously I'm very grateful,' said the King, 'but why? Why has he been doing these things?'

'Very complicated again sir,' said the tutor, 'and I'm not sure you would understand it, but I'll try.'

'And I'll try to understand it,' said the King.

'Well,' said the tutor, 'the Emperor is utterly opposed to the Great High Ruler and . . . and . . . .how shall I put it?'

'We're fighting his battles for him?' said the King.

'Exactly,' said the tutor, 'I knew you would see it clearly in the end.'

'It's been a very interesting lesson, tutor,' said the King.

'Thank you sir,' said the tutor.

THE MOON

'Tutor,' said the King, 'do you think that one day, we'll go to the moon?'

'Yes,' said the tutor, 'after all, God created it for us.'

'Did he?' said the King.

'Yes,' said the tutor, 'He created the large light and the small light. It's in Genesis.'

'Ah yes, of course,' said the King, 'so when we go there, it'll be ours.'

'Exactly,' said the tutor.

'But isn't there a man in the moon?' said the King.

'Well, people say there is,' said the tutor, 'but I don't think we need to bother about him.'

'But he is there,' said the King, 'so we'll have to negotiate with him, won't we?'

'Not really,' said the tutor, 'he's just a myth. Something that people say. He's just the 'Man in the Moon'. He could be anywhere and go anywhere: the Man on Mars. Or the Man on the Milky Way.'

'But what if he is there?' said the King.

'Then we can arrest him,' said the tutor.

'On what basis can we arrest him?' said the King.

'Because he's on our moon,' said the tutor, 'please do try to keep up, sir.'

'So when we go to the moon, we'll sort him out and the moon really will be ours?'

'Yes, indeed, sir,' said the tutor, 'there's no need to keep worrying about it. It's in the books: God created it and gave it to us.'

'Well that's all very reassuring,' said the King.

TALKING TO THE ENEMY

'Should we talk to the enemy?' said the King to his tutor.

'No,' said the tutor.

'I agree,' said the King, 'and yet . . . and yet . . . I have this nagging feeling that maybe, one day, far off, at some point, we'll have to.'

'Yes,' said the tutor, 'but that's so far off, and so far away, it's virtually the same as saying, "no, we shouldn't talk to the enemy".'

'So how do you see this thing ending?' said the King.

'Ending?' said the tutor, 'why are you talking about ending?'

'I just thought that at some point for the sake of all of us,' said the King, 'it would be a good idea for there to be an end.'

'Yes,' said the tutor, 'but we don't want an end where the enemy has any rights or powers to say anything.'

'Can you spell that out for me?' said the King.

'Well,' said the tutor, 'what it means is that if we can obliterate the enemy, we won't have to talk to the enemy, will we?'

'That's brilliant,' said the King, 'and so clear.'

'Thank you sir,' said the tutor.

'And should I be announcing something about this?' said the King.

'The best thing for you to say is: "There is no point in talking to the enemy because the enemy won't talk to us",' said the tutor.

'Would that be absolutely true?' said the King.

'Don't worry about that,' said the tutor, 'and I would also like you to add, "There is no point in talking to the enemy because the enemy wants to destroy us".'

'Good point,' said the King, 'though, it does occur to me that some might say, that we're a bit similar, in that we want to destroy them!'

'Yes,' said the tutor, 'but we're right and they're wrong. We're good people and they're bad people.'

'Of course,' said the King, 'I forgot that for the moment.'

'That's why we have these lessons, sir,' said the tutor.
'And I'm so grateful for them, tutor,' said the King.

THE EMPEROR'S JOB

'What actually is the Emperor's job?' said the King to his tutor.

'Good question,' said the tutor, 'and I'll try to answer it. The Emperor's job is to make sure that the Emperor's power and control carries on.'

'Fair enough,' said the King, 'and how does he do it?'

'Yes,' said the tutor, 'let's get down to basics. First thing he does is try to make sure that as many countries as is possible have Kings who think that he's a good and kind Emperor.'

'Just as we do,' said the King.

'Exactly,' said the tutor, 'and then, the Emperor backs people.'

'What's that?' said the King.

'Well,' said the tutor, 'if the Emperor thinks that this or that leader or group is going to help the Emperor's power and control to carry on, the Emperor sends them money and spears.'

'That's good,' said the King.

'Well, yes,' said the tutor, 'it is good, but the snag is that sometimes, that leader or group is not the leader or group that the Emperor likes anymore.'

'Oh dear,' said the King, 'what then?'

'The Emperor backs someone else to get rid of that leader or group,' said the tutor.

'You mean that the leader or group he was backing, is now the leader or group that he tries to get rid of?' said the King.

'Exactly,' said the tutor.

'But don't people point this out and say that the Emperor is being inconsistent or hypocritical?' said the King.

'They do,' said the tutor.

'What then?' said the King.

'We call people who say those things about the Emperor, traitors and subversives,' said the tutor.

'And that deals with them?' said the King.

'Mostly, yes,' said the tutor.

'Marvellous,' said the King, 'but what about the scribes?'

'Ah the scribes,' said the tutor, 'no problem there. The scribes say, "We are realists!" and that all things considered the Emperor is probably right.'

'And that the traitors are traitors?' said the King.

'Of course,' said the tutor.

'And life goes on,' said the King.

'Indeed it does,' said the tutor.

PEOPLE IN THE WAY

'There are some people,' said the King to his tutor, 'who technically aren't the enemy, because they're not armed.'

'That's correct,' said the tutor, 'but though they're not armed, they are in the way.'

'In the way of what?' said the King.

'In the way of us,' said the tutor.

'How do you mean?' said the King.

'They're in the way of where we want to be,' said the tutor.

'We want to be where they are?' said the King.

'That's it,' said the tutor.

'So what are we doing about it?' said the King.

'We're making sure that they're not there,' said the tutor.

'But how?' said the King.

'We have various ways,' said the tutor. 'Sometimes they're in the way when we're throwing our spears at the enemy soldiers. We warn them but people are very selfish about wanting to hang on to their homes and farms. And sometimes we move them. And sometimes, sadly, we have to throw our spears at them.'

'This sounds very practical,' said the King, 'what does the Emperor say about this?'

'It's his idea,' said the tutor, 'he did it years ago in his country. And he thinks it's a great idea if we do it in ours.'

'Oh that's good,' said the King, 'it's good to get backing from him.'

'No, I don't think you have that quite right,' said the tutor, 'he thinks it's a great idea so that he knows that his rule spreads wider and further than it did before.'

'So when we're getting rid of the "people in the way",' said the King, 'really we're doing it for him.'

'That's it,' said the tutor, 'it suits us, it suits him. It's what's called a

"coincidence of interest".'
    'Oh,' said the King, 'you're very good with these phrases, tutor.'
    'I know,' said the tutor.

BAD SCRIBES

'What do you think of scribes, tutor?' said the King to his tutor.
'Some of them are good, some of them are bad,' said the King's tutor.
'Fair enough,' said the King.
'No,' said the tutor, 'not fair enough.'
'How do you mean?' said the King.
'As I said,' said the tutor, 'some of them are bad,'
'Well,' said the King, 'if they're bad, they're bad. So what? If they're bad, no will bother to read them.'
'And that's where you're wrong,' said the tutor, ' a bad scribe is not a scribe who writes badly. A bad scribe is a scribe who makes us look bad.'
'Ah,' said the King, 'I hadn't thought of that. So is there anything we should do about these bad scribes?'
'Yes,' said the tutor.
'What?' said the King.
'Kill them,' said the tutor.
'Oh,' said the King, 'won't people object?'
'Of course,' said the tutor.
'So what do we do about that?' said the King.
'We say they were enemy soldiers,' said the tutor, 'and we're allowed to kill them.'
'Ah yes,' said the King, 'that makes sense.'
'Glad you see it that way,' said the tutor.

PEACE TREATY

'Good to see that we've signed the peace treaty, tutor,' said the King to his tutor.

'Indeed, sir,' said the King's tutor, 'I've been working on it for months.'

'Have you?' said the King, 'I had no idea. Why's it taken so long?'

'It's a very complex matter,' said the tutor, 'you don't need to bother your head about it.'

'No, no,' said the King, 'I'd really like to know.'

'Well,' said the tutor, 'to tell the truth, it was all worked out months ago.'

'Oh! Was it?' said the King, 'So why wasn't it implemented straightaway?'

'Because we didn't want the war to stop, sir,' said the tutor.

'But I thought you said it was our enemy who didn't want the war to stop,' said the King.

'Yes, sir,' said the tutor, 'we say that sort of stuff so that the scribes write it down and everyone thinks that it's the enemy who is unreasonable and we're reasonable.'

'Very good,' said the King, 'cunning! I like that. But even so, surely it would have been a good idea to stop the war. After all, we lost quite a few of our archers and pikemen.'

'There's one bit about this that you don't understand, sir,' said the tutor, 'we've found that if we have to make the choice between peace and war, we've found that mostly being at war is the better option.'

'So this treaty?' said the King, 'Is it a peace treaty or a war treaty?'

'It's a treaty for the time being,' said the tutor, 'while we work out our objectives.'

'What does the Emperor say about this?' said the King.

'Good point,' said the tutor, 'the new Emperor is a little unpredictable, but all we know at the moment is that he likes redrawing maps.'

'Sounds good,' said the King, 'and the enemy? Have we got rid of the enemy?'

'Not entirely,' said the tutor, 'but we're getting there.'
'All good,' said the King, 'shall we have breakfast?'
'That would be nice,' said the tutor.

LONG-TERM OBJECTIVES

'So we have the peace treaty,' said the King to his tutor, 'what about our long-term objectives?'

'Good point, sir,' said the King's tutor, 'and I'm glad to see you using a technical term like that.'

'So?' said the King, 'have our long-term objectives changed?'

'No,' said the tutor.

'But surely,' said the King, 'with this peace treaty we're going to have to come to all sorts of agreements with the people in the way.'

'People in the way?' said the tutor.

'You know,' said the King, 'the people in the way of us achieving our long-term objectives.

'Oh yes,' said the tutor. 'Them! But no, we go on making sure that we don't give in to the demands of the people in the way.'

'But won't the Emperor say that we have to?' said the King.

'What the Emperor says and what the Emperor does,' said the tutor, 'are two completely different things.'

'So we have the peace treaty,' said the King, 'we stop firing our arrows at each other for a while, but we press on with making sure that the people in the way are not in the way?'

'Yes,' said the tutor, 'but now we have to stop the war for a while, we go back to doing it, little by little.'

'That's marvellous,' said the King. 'Drink?'

'Thank you, sir,' said the tutor.

HIGHLY MORAL PEOPLE

'I've been reading what scribes have been saying about us in other countries,' said the King to his tutor.

'Me too' said the tutor, 'Do you have any favourites, sir?'

'Yes,' said the King, 'the ones who say that they are "unapologetic supporters". Did you like those?'

'Yes and no,' said the tutor. 'I find them a bit obvious and a bit crude. Good that they agree with us but not so good for winning support in those countries.'

'Really?' said the King, 'which ones did you like, then?'

'I like the ones written by highly moral people, people who talk about morality and fairness and humanity,' said the tutor.

'You surprise me there, tutor,' said the King, 'I've known you sometimes to be a bit dubious about morality.'

'I am,' said the tutor, 'but we need people with high moral standards about everything going on in the world, apart from when it comes to what we're doing.'

'Don't people see that as a bit iffy?' said the King. 'It sounds like double standards.'

'Best not to use phrases like that,' said the tutor, 'the point is that these people with high moral standards are not expressing anger towards us and what we do, they direct it at the people who object to what we're doing.'

'That sounds very useful,' said the King.

'It is,' said the tutor, 'and it sounds so very moral. That's what convinces people in these other countries.'

'Tea?' said the King.

'Not just now,' said the tutor, 'must dash.'

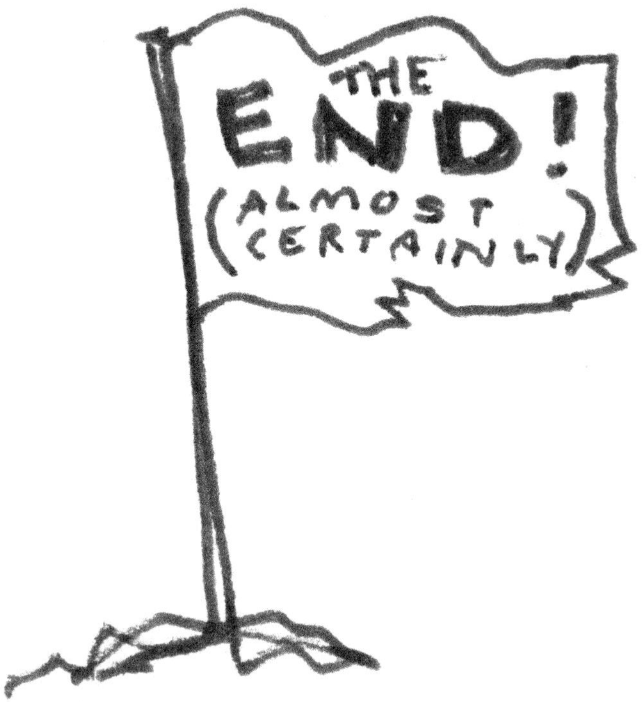
THE
END!
(ALMOST
CERTAINLY)

Other Books by Michael Rosen

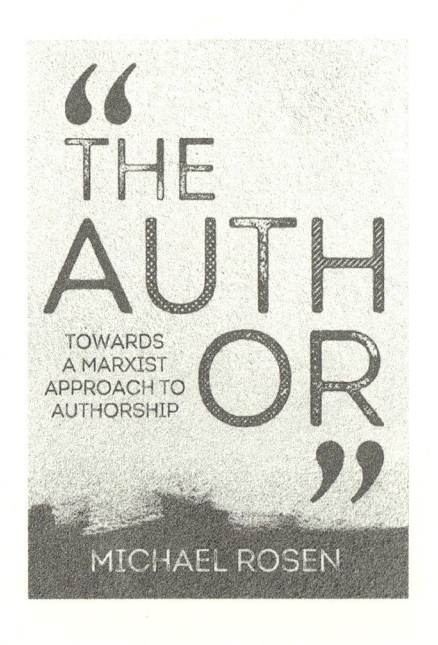

In 1997 I completed a Ph.D. on the subject of authoring a piece of children's literature – a book of poems that was eventually published as *You Wait Till I'm Older Than You* (Puffin). In the thesis I tried to put to one side mystical and Romantic ideas around creating poetry and instead, locate the whole process in reality.

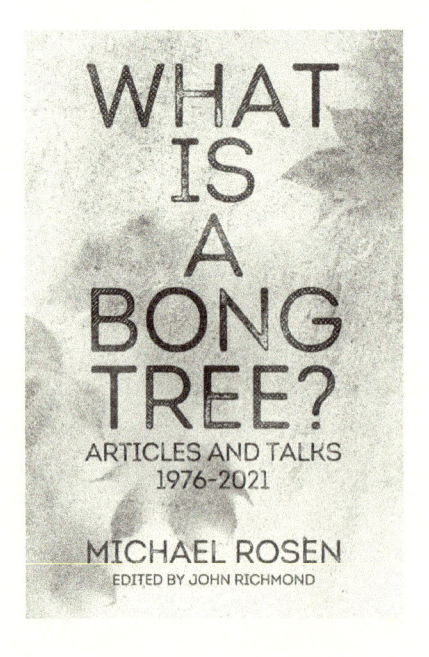

"This book brings together a big selection of Michael Rosen's writings and talks over five decades. They are about the centrality of literature, including children's literature, in the lives of all of us; about the power of poetry to inspire, console and entertain; and about the need to argue and campaign for these liberating forces in the face of ignorant and reductionist actions by successive governments in the United Kingdom."

John Richmond, Editor

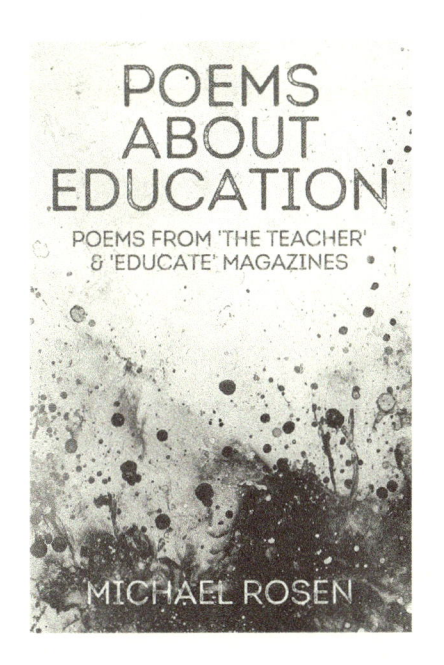

Poems About Education is a collection of poems that Michael Rosen has been writing for the magazines of the former National Union of Teachers and now the amalgamated union, the National Education Union. They are a mix of punchy, satirical, regretful, and a call to action, but always sharp, to the point and full of ironic observation.

This booklet gathers together some recent talks and blogs on writing and reading, for use by teachers, librarians, parents, or anyone interested in engaging children and students in reading and writing, analysing why and how we do both.

POETRY AND STORIES FOR PRIMARY AND LOWER SECONDARY SCHOOLS

MICHAEL ROSEN

This is a short guide for teachers on how to teach poetry – reading, responding and writing. It is full of ideas on where and how to start, descriptions of why it's such a valuable activity. It's for you to use, adapt and change as you think best for the school and students you have in front of you.

WRITING FOR PLEASURE

MICHAEL ROSEN

This booklet is the third in a series about reading, writing and responding to literature. It focuses on how to make writing pleasurable and interesting and would be ideal as part of teacher training, staff discussion, curriculum development or just for reading and using.

READING FOR PLEASURE

MICHAEL ROSEN

This is a short guide for teachers on how to help a school put in place a reading for pleasure policy. To support this policy the guide also takes a close look at how children read – what do they think as they read? I've also included some plans from teachers putting reading for pleasure policies in place. It's for you to use, adapt and change as you think best for the school and students you have in front of you.

MICHAEL ROSEN'S POETRY VIDEOS: HOW TO GET CHILDREN WRITING AND PERFORMING POEMS TOO

JONNY WALKER
WITH
MICHAEL ROSEN

This is a guide for teachers on how to support children to write and perform poems that matter to them – it shares creative ways to harness the classroom potential of the 'Kids' Poems and Stories with Michael Rosen' YouTube channel. It is a practical and supportive handbook, put together by a practising teacher, and it suggests some ways that fellow teachers can create enriching writing communities with and for their students.

Further details on all these self-published books, including where they can be ordered from, can be found on my website:

www.michaelrosen.co.uk/books

www.ingramcontent.com/pod-product-compliance
Ingram Content Group UK Ltd.
Pitfield, Milton Keynes, MK11 3LW, UK
UKHW040727190225
455309UK00003B/112